"Are You Seeing Anyone Seriously Right Now?"

Shelley asked softly.

David stared at her, thrown off course by her question. "What?"

"Do you have a girlfriend?"

He frowned, unable to see what *that* had to do with. "No. No one serious."

Her smile became more mischievous. "Then why won't you kiss me?"

"Because if we start something," he said, his voice low and husky, aching with need for her, "I'm going to have to finish it."

She reached up and put her hand over his, holding him to her. Her other hand lifted and flattened against his chest. "I could risk that," she whispered.

"Shelley..." He pulled her toward him, his pulse beating in his ears. "I'm not one of your upper-crust country-club lovers. I'm too rough around the edges for you, and you know it."

"I think I can handle it, David," she murmured, her lips only inches from his. "Try me."

Dear Reader,

Q. What does our heroine know about the hero when she first meets him?
A. Not much!

His personality, background, family—his entire life—is a total mystery. I started to think that the heroine never *truly* knows what's in store for her when she first sees the hero. In fact, *her* life from that moment on can be likened to an adventure with a "mysterious" man. And it's from these thoughts that our Valentine's Day promotion, MYSTERY MATES, was born. After all, who *is* this guy and what *is* he looking for?

Each of our heroes this month is a certain type of man, as I'm sure you can tell from the title of each February Desire book. The *Man of the Month* by Raye Morgan is *The Bachelor* . . . a man who never dreamed he'd have anything to do with—*children!* Cait London brings us *The Cowboy,* Ryanne Corey *The Stranger,* Beverly Barton *The Wanderer* and from Karen Leabo comes *The Cop.*

Peggy Moreland's hero, *The Rescuer,* is a very special man indeed. For while his story is completely fictitious, the photo on the cover is that of a Houston, Texas, fire fighter. Picked from a calendar the Houston Fire Department creates for charity, this man is truly a hero.

So, enjoy our MYSTERY MATES. They're sexy, they're handsome, they're lovable . . . and they're only from Silhouette Desire.

Lucia Macro
Senior Editor

RAYE MORGAN

THE BACHELOR

SILHOUETTE *Desire*

Published by Silhouette Books New York

America's Publisher of Contemporary Romance

SILHOUETTE BOOKS
300 East 42nd St., New York, N.Y. 10017

THE BACHELOR

Copyright © 1993 by Helen Conrad

ISBN: 0-373-05768-7

First Silhouette Books printing February 1993

All the characters in this book have no existence outside the imagination of the author and have no relation whatsoever to anyone bearing the same name or names. They are not even distantly inspired by any individual known or unknown to the author, and all incidents are pure invention.

Printed in the U.S.A.

Books by Raye Morgan

Silhouette Desire

Embers of the Sun #52
Summer Wind #101
Crystal Blue Horizon #141
A Lucky Streak #393
Husband for Hire #434
Too Many Babies #543
Ladies' Man #562
In a Marrying Mood #623
Baby Aboard #673
Almost a Bride #717
The Bachelor #768

Silhouette Romance

Roses Never Fade #427

RAYE MORGAN

favors settings in the West, which is where she has
spent most of her life. She admits to a penchant for
Western heroes, believing that whether he's a rugged
outdoorsman or a smooth city sophisticate, he tends
to have a streak of wildness that the romantic heroine
can't resist taming. She's been married to one of those
Western men for over twenty years and is busy raising
four more in her Southern California home.

A Letter from the Author

Dear Reader:

Dating—I can't remember if it was as fun as it was nerve-racking. One year I decided I was going to go after a handsome boy in my Spanish class. Gary was his name. I planned a whole campaign, and it was working. The only problem was, there was this other guy who kept getting in the way, making me laugh and asking me out. Finally, just to get rid of him, I agreed to go out. Once.

The strategy was to impress you at first in those days. Things usually went downhill from there, but on that first date, everything was special. Usually.

This guy, however, hadn't got the news. We picked up hamburgers at a take-out window, and the movie he chose was an hour away, out in the sticks—and a drive-in to boot. Remember drive-ins? But somehow it worked, and instead of being offended, I couldn't help but like him. He was funny and cute and cuddly, and we got lost driving home, and when he stood at my door and kissed me good night, he said, "You may not believe this, but you know what? I'm going to marry you." And I pulled back the curtain and watched him drive away and thought he was crazy.

We just celebrated our twenty-fifth wedding anniversary this year. We never go to the drive-in anymore, but he's still cuddly and funny and crazy. And I have no idea what ever happened to good old Gary.

Sincerely,

Raye Morgan

One

The phone call came at the worst possible time.

The small café was almost empty. Only beautiful, provocative Mia was lingering, flirting with David for all she was worth.

A guy couldn't help but feel flattered, he decided. The afternoon stretched out ahead of him, long and pleasantly full of possibilities.

It had already been a long day. Restaurant work was an interesting change from his usual career, but it wasn't exactly relaxing. He could certainly use a break. And lovely Mia with her long red hair and her full red lips seemed ideal for the task.

They'd been eyeing each other for almost a week and a half, ever since he'd arrived in Puerto Vallarta for his yearly visit. His two weeks were almost up. If anything was going to come of this, it was time to make a move.

He'd been hesitating. Funny. That was hardly like him. He was a man who liked women. In other years, his visits to this Mexican seacoast resort had been crammed full of romance. This time the girls who had hung around, giggling and batting eyelashes at him, had seemed suddenly young and silly. He'd found himself spending the late evenings talking into the night with Rosa, the middle-aged waitress who'd worked here for twenty-five years, instead of whispering sweet nothings into young, shell-like ears.

But tonight was going to be different. Mia was beautiful. She didn't giggle. Her green eyes flashed with promises of erotic danger and her glances fairly burned with sensual heat. This was a little too much to resist. And he'd never been a martyr.

David put down the stack of dirty plates he was carrying, pulled off the apron and sat down at the table with his tantalizing visitor, laughing at something she'd said. She eyed him with a sultry look.

"I do, too, have a tattoo there," she claimed archly. "Want to see?"

Did he want to see? David grinned. This was better. He was getting in the mood, all right. "I've always been a patron of the arts," he said. "I wouldn't miss it for the world."

Mia was reaching for the elastic neckline of her cotton blouse, when the world put in its own claim with the annoying ring of the telephone. David glanced at Mia, who was already baring one very lovely shoulder and about to go for more, and then he looked at the telephone. Every male instinct he possessed told him to ignore the call and reach for Mia. Yet there was something especially insistent about this ringing. It was one of those crucial moments on which the rest of his life might hinge. The lady or the tiger. Instant gratification or destiny.

He never could figure out what made him go for the phone.

"Just a second," he told Mia, rising from his chair and turning toward the counter where the old-fashioned black telephone sat. "Hold that thought."

Mia pouted, but he picked up the receiver, anyway.

"Hello?" he said impatiently.

The feminine voice on the other end of the line was smoky, whispery, like silk and candlelight, and it got his attention right away.

"David Coronado?"

His eyes narrowed. She sounded like a femme fatale from an old detective movie. "Yes?"

"Is this the David Coronado who was stationed in Germany with Reed Brittman ten years ago?"

His hand tightened on the receiver. The voice was mesmerizing, and yet there was a sense of tension in it that set the hair up on the back of his neck. "Yes," he said quickly. "Who's this?"

"Oh, I'm so glad I found you."

He was glad, too, but he had to know more. "*Who* are you?"

"David, you don't know me, but I have to ask a favor...."

A man's voice sounded in the room where she was speaking from, and she gasped softly, whispered "Oh, no" and the line went dead.

David stood for a moment with the receiver pressed to his ear, as though she might come back if he only waited long enough. Someone had come up behind her and either frightened her into hanging up or...

"David."

Mia was calling him. He turned and looked at her, his eyes blank. The prospect of playing hide-and-seek for Mia's tattoos had suddenly lost its former appeal. His mind was consumed with the call he'd just received.

Who was she? She had to know Reed. He and Reed had been army buddies, but that had been years ago. Why had she called? What had just happened to her?

All he could think about was that incredibly sensual voice. It filled his head. He'd felt it as much as heard it. And somehow he was sure she would be calling back.

Making an excuse, he bid Mia and her tattoo an urgent farewell, and shooed her out the door. Then he went about the business of setting up for the evening meal. The café was homey and old-fashioned, just like Maya and Eduardo, his grandparents who owned the place. Every year at this time he came down from San Diego to help them out, give them some time to escape on vacation for a couple of weeks. This year they were visiting friends in Guadalajara while he was slinging hash—or rather frijoles—back here in Puerto Vallarta. The café was a favorite of the locals, though far removed from the flashier tourist trade down by the beach. David enjoyed coming every year. It was a change of pace from Southern California.

But he wasn't thinking about that now. His attention was all on the silent telephone.

"Ring," he ordered aloud. "Ring, damn you."

And it did.

He lunged for it.

"Hello. David?"

A current went through him at the sound of her voice. What was it about this woman?

"Yes, this is David. What happened? Are you all right?"

"I'm fine." She was whispering, so she was obviously still in danger, wherever she was.

"Who are you?" he asked impatiently.

"I'm Reed Brittman's sister, Shelley."

"Shelley." So that was the connection. He recognized the name, but he couldn't put a face to it. "Have we ever met?"

"No. But Reed has talked about you for years. And when he found out I was coming down here to Puerto Vallarta, he gave me your number in case..."

"In case you needed help?" His fingers curled around the receiver. Reed's sister needed help. He would do anything for Reed, so naturally, he would do anything for his sister. More to the point, he would do anything for a woman with a voice like that.

"Where are you? Do you want me to come and get you? Are you in trouble?"

"I... I'm sort of trapped here."

That was what he'd been afraid of. Someone had her somewhere she didn't want to be. No matter. He'd take care of it.

"Where? Give me an address and I'll be right over."

"No." Her voice rose a bit. "Oh, no, that wouldn't work. It would only make things worse."

He frowned. "What things? What's he doing to you?"

"I... David, not so fast. I didn't say anyone was doing anything to me."

"I heard a man's voice. And you say you're trapped."

Her sigh was as lovely as her words. "I have to handle this on my own."

He didn't like the sound of that. "Shelley, I want to help you, but if you won't tell me where you are..."

She was laughing softly. "David, you're just as nice as I knew you would be."

Nice? His head went back and he flexed his wide shoulders. He didn't want to be nice. He wanted to be tough and mean and slay a dragon for her. That voice. He knew she was beautiful. He could hear it.

"Where are you?" he demanded roughly.

"Never mind that. I just want to know if I can count on you. I think I can get away tonight, but it will be late. Where will you be?"

"Right here. I'm staying in an apartment above a café." He quickly gave her the address. "It's up the hill from the Playa del Oro, in the residential section."

"Then it's not far from the marina."

"Just a few blocks." He frowned. "Is that where you are, at the marina?"

"Never mind that. I'll find you."

He didn't like this, but she wasn't going to give. "I'll leave the outside entrance unlocked."

She paused. "Will that be safe?" she asked.

"Of course. Puerto Vallarta is a nice, friendly town."

"Is it?" Her voice was wistful. "I guess I haven't seen that side of it."

Adrenaline was coursing through him. Someone had been hurting her somehow, and he wanted that person to pay. At the same time he had to laugh at himself. He'd never met the woman face to face, and he wanted to be her protector. This was crazy.

"Do you have a way to get here? A car?"

"I'll take care of that. Don't worry." She paused as though listening for something, and when she spoke again, her voice was muffled, as though she'd put her hand over the mouthpiece. "Thanks, David. You're a lifesaver."

The way she said his name gave him goose bumps. "Shelley, tell me where you are," he urged. "If something happens..."

"I can't tell you, David." Her voice lowered to a sexy whisper that almost made him writhe. "Wait for me. I'll be late, but I'll be there."

And she was gone.

David felt as though he'd been running hard and needed to catch his breath. He hung up slowly and stared into space. Shelley Brittman. Funny how names from the past came back to haunt you.

Her brother Reed had been his best buddy in the army. Ten years ago, the two of them had explored Germany together, the landmarks as well as the nightlife. And when they'd shipped back to the States, Reed had invited him up to his family's house in the Hamptons for a few days.

David had had no idea what to expect. He'd known Reed's family had to be well-off from things he'd observed and the schools Reed had gone to. But he'd been stunned by what he'd found himself in the midst of—polo ponies, benefits for the ballet, portraits of famous American patriots from the Revolutionary War among the family tree, heads of major industries over for tennis on the family courts, politicians he'd seen on the evening news dropping by for dinner. The Brittmans were big-time and old money. The longer he'd stayed, the smaller and stranger he'd felt. He'd been in alien territory, and he didn't know the language.

He'd left as soon as he could escape, and despite other invitations, he never went back. But it hadn't taken long for his relationship with Reed to regain its former warmth. They still kept in touch. In fact, Reed made it a point to drop by and see him at least once a year, when he was in California on business. They would always be friends. But David knew that could only work on neutral ground. The Brittmans were just too exalted a family for him to stomach.

And now their daughter was coming to him for help. Shelley—thinking hard he could remember a few things Reed had said about her now and then. Wasn't she married to some wealthy Greek tycoon? He'd had the impression that the marriage hadn't lasted. But never having met Shelley, anything Reed might have said about her hadn't stuck in his mind. He had some vague idea that she'd always been regarded as something of a frivolous bubblehead. But that didn't describe the woman he'd been talking to on the telephone.

What was she running from? He supposed he would find out soon enough. He only wished he had been able to find out where she was. He didn't like the idea of her trying to get here by herself. But he didn't have much choice in the matter now. All he could do was wait.

Rosa Sanchez had worked as a waitress in David's grandparents' restaurant since before he could remember. She was like an aunt to him. And she treated him like her favorite charitable cause.

"Querido," she announced as she flounced into the café a short time before the dinner hour. "I have found the girl for you."

Looking up from the salmon filets he was slicing, David groaned. "Again?"

She posed, looking at him reproachfully, her huge gold earrings swaying. "No, this time she is perfect. She's educated, cultured, and so very, very pretty."

David grinned. He'd been here before. "And she's also your cousin, right?"

She shrugged grandly. "Of course. I have many cousins, my dear." Rosa started to fill the salt shakers, but she kept right on talking as she worked. "She's a legal secretary on a consulting basis. She works with the most powerful lawyers and businessmen in town. She speaks three languages fluently."

Naturally. All the women Rosa found for him were paragons of virtue. "And is incredibly beautiful," David supplied helpfully.

Rosa stopped and placed a hand over her heart. "I swear on my sainted mother's head, she is gorgeous."

David grinned. "Your idea of gorgeous doesn't always coincide with mine. Remember the bald trapeze artist?"

Rosa shook her head balefully. "Who knew, sweetheart? When I met her, she wore a wig."

David shrugged, and she went on.

"Anyway, she is gorgeous, and her body is still good, too, even after the three kids...."

He reacted to that one. "Whoa, wait a minute. Three kids?"

"But don't you see, that is what is so perfect. She's not one of these flighty young things like these girls that hang around here every afternoon during *siesta*, trying to tempt you into doing naughty things."

He pretended to be shocked. "Rosa!"

She tossed her dark, curling hair and looked at him grimly. "I know what goes on. Do you think I'm blind? No, Sandra is not like those girls. She's mature, she's seen the world—"

"She's divorced."

Rosa hesitated. "Not exactly. Her husband has...sort of disappeared. And she has these three lovely children...."

David packed away the filets and turned to survey the café, mentally going over the checkpoints, making sure things were prepared for the opening, which was only moments away. The counter was clean, the ketchup bottles and taco sauce jars refilled. Fresh blossoms from his grandmother's rose garden decorated every one of the five little tables. Everything looked just as his grandparents would want it to, just as it had looked for all the years he could remember.

"Well, she's already broken my number-one rule," he drawled in an aside to Rosa, grinning as he passed behind her and dropped a kiss on her cheek. "No kids."

Rosa reached for her apron. It was almost time to unlock the door. She'd been doing this for so many years, she could sense the time and didn't even have to look at a clock. "But only one actually lives with her," she went on cajoling earnestly. "The other two are in reform school...."

David couldn't help but laugh. "Rosa! Reform school? You want to saddle me with a woman whose kids are already in reform school?"

She gazed at him dolefully, shaking her head. "*Hijo,* you're becoming hard and cold and selfish." She shook her finger at him. "In other words, a typical bachelor."

"The hard and selfish I can agree with," he muttered more to himself than to her as he started toward the front door. "But cold—" his mouth twisted as he thought of Shelley's voice and its effect on him "—no, I don't think so."

Rosa wasn't giving up quite yet. "But just think," she called after him. "If you marry Sandra, your future is assured. You won't have to go back to San Diego. You can stay here, take over the café when your grandparents retire...."

He turned back, laughing. "So we finally get down to it. This is all a plot to solidify your own job security. Is that it?"

She turned away proudly, disdaining to answer such an absurd charge. But she turned back and watched him as he went to the door, unlocked it and greeted the first customers of the evening. For all their comfortable bantering, she did worry about him. She loved him like one of her own. She could still remember the wary, guarded child who used to come to stay with his grandparents every summer, the boy who was warm and loving to those who knew him best, but cocky and arrogant to the outside world. He hadn't been too many steps away from reform school himself, now and then.

He was different now—handsome, successful and self-assured with his dark eyes and his wide shoulders. The bloodlines of his ancestors, Aztecs and Castilians, Kansas pioneers and Irish horsemen, all combined to produce a man as strong and noble as any she'd ever seen. But every now and then she got a glimpse of something that reminded her of that scared little boy. He still lived inside David, some-where deep and hidden.

"What he needs is a good woman," she murmured, watching him laugh with two pretty young things as he showed them to a table. "Why won't he let himself fall in love?"

Two

The evening seemed to drag like no other evening he'd ever endured. He spent more time looking at the clock than preparing meals. Rosa had to remind him twice about a certain double order of seviche.

But finally the last customer left and Rosa went home, still talking about her cousin Sandra as she walked out the door. David cleaned up, made the routine preparations for the next day and closed down the place.

He'd left the outside entrance door unlocked and he half hoped Shelley would be upstairs when he got there, but the apartment was empty. He checked the door; it was unlocked. He stared out into the night and wished he had some idea of where she was. He could still hear her voice in his head. She was in danger. He was sure of it. He couldn't stay here and wait, knowing that. He had to do something. If only he had some idea of where to find her.

The marina. She'd said something about that. And the telephone connection had been full of static, as though she'd been calling from a ship phone. Grabbing a light jacket, he raced down the outside stairway and folded his long body into his small sports car. The ride to the marina only took a few minutes. He cruised the place for a quarter of an hour, but he didn't see anything that would make him think she was there. Detouring off on every side street, he rode slowly back home. There wasn't a sign of her. He was beginning to wonder if he'd made her up in his head.

The apartment was still empty. He paced through the simple two-room space for over an hour, then lost patience with himself. "You don't even know this woman," he lectured himself out loud. "She probably won't show up. And if she does, she'll look like Reed with longer hair and glasses." He squinted, making himself see that picture.

But he couldn't convince himself to stop waiting for her, until the clock struck two in the morning and he decided he had to get some sleep. He took a shower, more to calm himself down than anything else, and when he stepped out, slipping into a robe and humming to himself, he thought he heard something.

Stopping, he listened. No. There was no one there. It was all in his head. She wasn't coming, and he was a fool to care. He pulled open the bathroom door, stepped into the bedroom and found that he was dead wrong. There was someone there, all right. In fact, there were two someones. Two very young someones.

"Hi, mister," said one of them, a little girl with sandy blond hair in braids and freckles on her turned-up nose. She and a little boy were sitting at the foot of David's bed, swinging their feet, their huge eyes trained on his every move.

"Uh, hi, guys," David replied unsteadily, thrown completely off guard. He blinked at them, not sure whether he might be seeing things. "What's new?"

The little boy piped up. "Mama told us to stay here. She said, 'Don't move.'"

"I see." He glanced at the little girl. She looked older than the boy, maybe six or seven to his four or five. "Where did she go, exactly?"

"She'll be back in a minute," the little boy interjected. "That's what she said. In a minute."

The little girl nodded but didn't say another word. They both looked at him expectantly. After all, he was the adult. He would know what to do next.

But he had no idea. Kids. He didn't know a thing about them. He hadn't talked to any since he'd been a kid himself, and that was a time he didn't much like to remember.

Don't show any fear, he told himself silently. Hadn't he heard somewhere that they could sense fear, just like dogs? His experience with children was nil. For all he knew, they barked and fetched, as well.

Their mother had to be Reed's sister. At least, he certainly hoped so. If this was just some new random group of visitors, he was going to have a very busy night.

"What are you two doing here?" he asked at last, still puzzled by that one.

They stared at him wide-eyed.

"Mama said you are going to baby-sit us," the little girl said at last.

The concept hit him like a sock on the chin. "I'm going to what?"

No, no. That wasn't the deal. One beautiful damsel in distress with a husky voice was the deal he'd signed on for. Nothing had been said about a pair of ragtag kids who needed to be looked after every moment.

He reacted like any other red-blooded male confronted with such an unwelcome prospect. "I can't do it," he protested quickly. "I'm no baby-sitter."

They both nodded solemnly in unison.

"Mama said."

That was obviously the last word on any subject. For just a moment he had a panicked nightmare vision. What if she'd left these kids with him? What if she wasn't coming back at all?

"Where is she?" he asked, looking around as though she might spring at him and yell "boo" at any given moment.

"She went back down to get the suitcase," the little boy told him solemnly. "We had to leave it on a corner 'cuz it got too heavy."

David looked at him levelly. It sounded like a ploy to him. If she didn't show up in another few minutes...

But there was a sound at the door, and then she was in the room, a small suitcase in her hand.

"Hi," she said breathlessly. "Sorry about this."

He turned and looked at her, and time stood still. He'd been telling himself for hours that she would never look as good as she sounded, and he'd been right. She looked even better.

Her hair still caught the moonlight from the open doorway. It settled around her shoulders like a lacy piece of midnight mist she might have picked up as she came through the dark. Silvery blonde. It looked like spun satin, light as a breeze.

Her eyes were the kind of blue he'd seen on antique Chinese silk, dark and luminous and studded with stars. Her body was slender, her movements a little too quick, impatient. She had her shoulders set with quiet determination, and there was anxiety in her pretty face, but all the same, there was a sense that laughter was about to bubble up from just below the surface.

She didn't look like Reed at all. David felt tongue-tied—like a ten-year-old with his first crush—as she came toward him, her hand outstretched with the quick, casual self-confidence one only got through breeding.

"I'm Shelley Brittman," she said. "And you are a saint."

He took her hand and tried not to look as foolish as he felt, standing there in his robe. His eyes met hers, but he couldn't hold the gaze. It was like staring into the sun.

"Are these yours?" he asked, nodding toward the children.

Her natural grin was a little strained around the edges, but still serviceable. "Guilty as charged. I hope they haven't been bothering you."

"Not at all." He hesitated, looking down at her hand as she finally pulled it away again. No wedding ring, he noted, then frowned to make up for the thought. He was still reeling from the way she looked, the way she sounded. He'd expected to enjoy this. He hadn't expected to be overwhelmed, and he wasn't sure he liked it.

"I didn't realize you would come with accessories."

"Oh, didn't I mention the kids when I spoke to you on the phone?" She looked genuinely surprised. "Sorry. This is Jill and this is Chris. We come as a set, I'm afraid." That radiant smile again. "Children, this is David Coronado, your Uncle Reed's best friend in the whole world."

What could he say? Solemnly, he shook hands with the children, and they shook hands back, and then bounced on the bed. He frowned again, looking at them. Did they ever stop moving?

She glanced at him sideways, seeming to sense his misgivings. "Is this the only bedroom?" she asked, looking around.

He nodded. "You three will have to share the bed. There's a couch out on the landing over the café. I'll use that."

Her slender hand flashed in the air between them. "Never. We'll take the couch. Or the floor. Just give us some blankets. We'll do fine. We are not going to kick you out of your own bed."

He turned to look at her, still stunned by the way she looked, the way she sounded. He knew he was staring at her, but something kept telling him she couldn't possibly be the genuine article. She was like something out of an adolescent dream. And everybody knew you couldn't trust dreams.

"Take the bed," he said rather more gruffly than was necessary, but that was to try to cover up the way she threw him off balance. "Of course you'll take the bed."

She looked at him uncertainly for a moment. Then, as though she'd read something in his eyes, she nodded. "All right. Thank you very much."

Her gaze dropped to take in his bare legs, and suddenly he was very conscious of how naked he was under the flimsy robe.

"Uh, I'll get something on," he muttered, turning back into the tiny bathroom. He pulled the door, but not all the way, so he could still talk to her.

"There are extra blankets in the closet. And more pillows, too." He dropped the robe and pulled on his slacks, but his shirt was wadded up on the floor, soaking up water from his shower. There was no hope there. He emerged again, shirtless and barefoot. "And plenty of fresh towels on the shelf under the sink in the bathroom," he said.

He turned and looked at her in time to catch the slight widening of her eyes as she took in his muscular chest and the way his stomach flattened, washboard tight, where it disappeared beneath his belt. For just a moment he wasn't

sure what that hot feeling in his face was. And then he realized he was blushing.

Blushing. He was a thirty-year-old man with a wealth of
experience with women, and he was blushing because this
one had let him know with one fleeting glance that he was
sexually attractive. What was the matter with him? Was he
losing his mind?

He took a deep breath and glanced at the case she'd gone
back for. "How did you get here?" he asked, working hard
to keep his voice low. He had a quick fear of hearing it
crack, like it used to when he was fourteen.

"We walked."

"You walked?" It was over a mile to the nearest tourist
area, and half a mile from the marina. But all of that was
down at sea level. It was quite a climb to his grandparents'
restaurant. "All the way up that hill with those two kids in
tow?"

She hesitated, her eyes clouding. "I didn't dare take a cab.
He...he could have traced where we had gone and I couldn't
take that chance," she admitted nervously.

David stared at her, wondering what to believe. His first
reaction was to think that this lady had been watching too
much television. "Who is *he?*" he asked softly.

She glanced at where the children were bouncing on the
bed, shaking her head, and he got the message. She didn't
want to talk about it in front of the kids. Well, that was all
right with him. But she was going to have to talk about it
sometime.

She turned and picked up the little suitcase, dropping it
on the bed. He watched her and wondered about the odd
fluttering he was feeling in the pit of his stomach. She was
wearing a powder blue jumpsuit in some sort of fabric that
looked like cashmere, with soft ballerina flats on her feet.
When she moved, her hair settled around her every time,

like something out of an animated movie. He couldn't shake the feeling that she couldn't possibly be real.

"I brought along a few of the children's clothes, but I couldn't get to any of my things." She flipped open the case and pulled out some brightly colored pajamas. "You don't happen to have any spare nightgowns around, do you?"

The thought of her in a nightgown did strange things to his sense of balance, and he leaned against the wall, trying to be casual and stop swaying in the breeze at the same time.

"Sorry. The only person who ever uses this apartment is me, when I come down to visit my grandparents."

She looked up at him and smiled. "Reed said that you come down periodically. And when I told him we were going to Mexico he gave me your address and phone number—just in case. I guess I'm really lucky you happened to be here just when I needed you."

Lucky. He wasn't sure if that was the right word for it. He wanted to smile at her, but he couldn't. He felt like the boy with his finger in the dike. If he relaxed, if he let himself go, even a little bit, he might turn into a gushing idiot and start drooling all over her. He had to keep his guard up.

But that didn't mean he couldn't try to be hospitable. "Listen, you can use one of my shirts, if you want to."

"Really?" She was smiling again and he wished she would quit it. "That would be great."

Good Lord, he was going to blush again. Softly and vehemently, he uttered an ugly four letter word and turned away. This was ridiculous. He was a man usually in control of himself and everything around him. He didn't like this feeling of helplessness. Damn it, he wasn't going to stand for it.

He turned back, his face as hard as he was going to force his heart to be. Shelley was looking at him curiously, but he paid no attention to that. He glanced from her to the children to the bed.

"Are all three of you going to be able to sleep in this narrow bed?" he asked, wishing he had something more luxurious to offer.

But she didn't seem to notice any lack. "Sure. We're used to it. They crawl in bed with me at night when they're scared all the time. Don't you?" she said to Jill and Chris.

The two children bounced up into her arms and she gave them a quick squeeze, laughing.

"Okay, first one in 'jamas gets to tell the good-night story."

Articles of clothing began to fly across the room, and David realized this was his cue to leave.

"I'll be right out here on the landing in case you need anything," he said, turning to go.

She nodded rather absently, watching her children. Then she looked up, gave him a quick smile and followed him out of the room.

"I do want to thank you again. It's so kind of you to take us in this way. I hope we haven't disrupted your life too much. Think of us as refugees from the storm."

He turned and looked down at her. He was beginning to get hold of himself again. She was pretty, but so what? She was just a woman, like any other woman: flesh and blood, virtues and faults, good days and bad days. And she was also asking for a lot of favors without handing back much information. It was time she set the record straight.

"Just exactly what are you a refugee from?" he asked evenly, searching her face for a hint of an answer.

"What?" Her eyes were blank.

He frowned. He didn't like being stonewalled. "What are you running from? What's got you so spooked?"

She stared right back at him, not backing down. "Who says I'm *spooked?*"

He leaned a little closer, his eyes hard as stones. "I say it, lady. You said something on the phone about being trapped. I can see you've been scared today. You're still on edge. Don't try to con me."

She licked her lips, a flash of anger appearing and then vanishing again quickly in the depths of her blue eyes. "I'm not trying to con you, David," she said quietly, using that voice again, almost like a weapon. "But I am going to protect my privacy."

He smiled, but there was more mockery in it than mirth. "Privacy is one of the first things you lose when you're on the run," he said coolly. "I still haven't figured out why you're running. Do you think this man you've...been with will come after you?"

She winced at the way he said *been with,* and he was almost sorry he'd put it that way. Almost, but not quite. It did annoy him to think of her with some sleaze she'd ended up having to run away from. She was Reed's sister, after all. She ought to take better care of herself—and her kids.

"Yes," she answered, accepting his terminology.

He shrugged. "Who is he? What's going on?"

There was no hesitation in her response. "I don't really want to talk about it."

His eyes hardened as he stared down at her. "And I don't want to go to bed not knowing."

She searched his eyes, her silvery blue gaze cool and assessing. Suddenly a wall seemed to slam into place. She lifted her chin and turned away.

"We're in the way here," she said crisply, turning back toward the room where her children were getting into bed. "I'm sorry. We'll pack back up and leave right away."

She started to march off, but he grabbed her by the shoulders and spun her around.

"What are you talking about?" he demanded, holding her firmly. "What's the matter?"

She glared at him defiantly, her indignation unleashed. "You don't want us here. You've made that plain enough."

Now where did she get a crazy idea like that? "That's not true," he said quickly. "That's not true at all."

Her eyes flashed. "Then why are you so angry?"

He blinked at her, surprised. Why was he so angry? Maybe *angry* wasn't the right word. *Bothered* was more like it.

"I'm not angry," he claimed, but his words rang a bit hollow. He had been acting gruffly and he knew it. He had to. It was a case of self-defense. His fingers loosened their hold on her shoulders and his face softened. "I'm sorry," he said quietly. "I didn't mean to come across like a jerk."

"Not a jerk." A smile tugged at the corners of her mouth. "Just an annoyed person."

He shook his head. "Listen, you're Reed's sister. My house is yours." He paused, releasing her, then continued. "But there's something going on. If I'm hiding you from someone, I think I have a right to know who and what I'm up against."

She nodded slowly, her eyes dark and mysterious. "You're right, of course." Her smile was strained. "But that still doesn't mean I'm going to go into it now. I'm really tired and I'm not up to explaining it all to you right now. You're going to have to give me some time. I have to sort it out in my own mind first." She hesitated, then faced him. "I'll just tell you this. Yes, I am running from a man. We were on his yacht in the marina. It became impossible to stay. I've got to get back to the States as quickly as possible."

"Without him knowing."

She pushed her hair back and suddenly she looked as tired as she claimed to be. "Yes. I have some business affairs to take care of in the morning. And then we'll be out of your hair."

Her blue eyes were clear and fearless, but they were also hiding something. Still, he knew he wasn't going to get any more information out of her tonight. He watched her disappear into the apartment and he groaned softly.

Bother. Yes, that was the word all right. She bothered him, rubbed him raw, turned him on, made him feel as loose as a lusting teenager. And he didn't like it at all.

She would be gone in mere hours. That was what he kept telling himself as he stripped out of the slacks and slipped beneath the sheet he'd put on the lumpy couch. She would be gone and life could go back to normal. Now if he could just get some sleep....

But sleep didn't come. He lay listening to the sounds of the three of them bedding down for the night, and when the noises ceased and he knew they were all out like lights, he still stared into the darkness, thinking about Shelley.

Was it because she was Reed's sister that she was having this tremendous effect on him? Was it the silken voice or the beautiful face? Was it the haunted look he saw in her eyes? Or the way she didn't back down?

"Mark all of the above," he muttered to himself, shifting his position and wondering, fleetingly, if he was going to get up with a very stiff back in the morning.

But this was all very strange. He'd heard her voice on the telephone and he'd gone out of his mind, like an idiot, like a crazy person.

He sighed, closing his eyes. He'd turned thirty this year. Maybe he was going through some sort of early mid-life crisis. It didn't make any sense for him to go into a tailspin because of Shelley Brittman. She was beautiful, sure, but so were a lot of other women. So was Mia, for Pete's sake.

But he had to admit, Shelley was different. She'd appeared like a vision in the night. She was exotic and romantic, and at the same time, she wasn't for him, and he knew it. To a guy who came from where he came from, her kind was poison. He didn't want her. He didn't want her at all. So why couldn't his libido quiet down and leave him alone?

Because no matter how much he tried to deny it, she knocked him out. TKO. No contest.

She was like a vision, ideal and untouchable. He'd never seen a woman before who came so close to perfection.

He suddenly remembered that he'd seen Shelley's room in the house in the Hamptons. Even ten years later the memory stuck with him. It had been a beautiful room. Perfect—all white and pink and lace—as though it had belonged to some storybook child who couldn't possibly be real. A perfect world for a perfect woman.

He remembered he'd been slightly repulsed by all that perfection, and had turned to go. His jacket had brushed against a porcelain figure of a dancer sitting on the corner of the low bookcase. Before he could catch it, it had crashed to the ground and smashed into a hundred sharp pieces of glass.

Reed's mother had been showing him the room. She'd been gracious, not letting on for a moment that his accident had caused her any annoyance. But two days later, as he was preparing to leave, he'd glanced in the room again, and there was a new porcelain figure, exactly like the old one. Everything obviously had to be perfect at all times.

What a contrast to his own world. Or should he say worlds? After all, he'd grown up in two of them—the large, loving, rambunctious family of his mother's midwestern clan, and the quieter, simpler life he'd lived in Los Angeles with his hard-working father, clinging to the edge of poverty. Neither world would have known what to make of a woman like Shelley, or the kind of life she'd led. No one ever kept a perfect bed for him, just in case he might want to revert back to childhood again. Just the thought of it made him smile in the dark.

But beautiful as she was, Shelley was no piece of brittle purity, no ice princess. There was flesh and blood beneath the lovely exterior and a vivacious flash of temper behind the sparkling blue eyes. And, he had no doubt, a reservoir of passion hidden just below the surface. The thought of making love with her set his heart pounding again. And he knew he had no right to think things like that.

Who was the man she was running from, anyway? Her husband? A lover? A woman as beautiful as Shelley would always have a man around.

A shutter banged. The wind off the ocean was picking up. It banged again and he threw back the covers, forcing himself to his feet. He walked softly through the apartment, moving to the window and latching the shutters to stop the noise. Then he turned to go back to his makeshift bed.

He hadn't meant to look at her. He'd done fine going in, walking right by the bed without a glance. But on his way back out, he couldn't resist.

She lay between her two children like a modern-day Madonna, her eyes closed, her breathing even. Something turned in his chest, like the twist of a knife, and he realized he was reaching for her, reaching out his hand to touch her golden hair. He jerked his hand back, repelled by his own impulses, and turned away.

It was worse than he'd thought. His body was playing traitor. He only hoped he could make it until he got the three of them off to the airport the next day without making a fool of himself.

Three

Someone was snoring. The snoring was rattling the bed. Shelley reached out groggily to push him, stop the snoring. But instead of a big, hard man, her fingers made contact with a skinny little backbone, the vertebrae sticking out like the spines on a dinosaur, and her eyes snapped open.

"Oh, Chris." She sighed, and gave his back a quick rub before turning to face her other child.

The room was barely beginning to get light. The sky she could see around the edges of the blinds in the window was purple. A new day.

"We're going home," she whispered, though both of her children slept. Stretching with a yawn, she smiled into the gloom. Home. It sure sounded good.

Slowly she assimilated her new reality. She was in Reed's friend's apartment, and she was running away from Armand. *Again.*

Fear tingled along the rough edges of her nerves. And that was new. She hadn't been afraid of Armand before. Now she knew she would never be able to trust him again.

What if they didn't make it home? What if he caught them?

Just days ago she would have scoffed at these qualms *and* she would have said to herself, what could he possibly do to us?

Now she knew.

She was lucky she'd had this place to run to. David made a great protector. He was big and strong and self-assured— she couldn't have found a better man if she'd tried. It was too bad he didn't like her, or anything about her. She knew he was going to be very happy to get rid of them. And she would oblige just as quickly as she possibly could.

But first she was going to need him to do some baby-sitting for her. She smiled, thinking of what his reaction was going to be to that idea. But she had very little choice. She couldn't take the children with her and there was no one else in Puerto Vallarta she could trust with her most precious cargo.

Sounds were filtering up from the café below. David was already awake and working downstairs. She slipped out from between her two sleeping children and made her way into the bathroom, washing her face and tying her hair up in a knot on the top of her head. She thought about putting the powder blue jumpsuit on again, and made a face. David was going to have to help her find something else to wear, something that Armand wouldn't know, something that would let her blend into the general population. A disguise.

The kids were still asleep when she emerged, and she decided to run down and ask David if he knew anyone she could borrow some clothes from.

She found a pair of shorts to slip into and then padded down the stairs, past the tall windows letting in the golden rays of the morning sun, and into the café.

He didn't see her at first. He was leaning over a huge kettle of soup, staring down into the murky depths as though he'd lost something in it. One strand of silky dark hair had fallen over his eyes. He wore a blue green print shirt over the chest that had looked so good glistening in the lamplight the night before, and tight, faded jeans over his muscular legs. He was a good-looking man. But it was the apron that made her smile. It seemed incongruous, this great big strapping man leaning over a hot stove, cooking.

"Good morning," she said, amusement in her voice.

He looked up and for just a moment, she saw the real David Coronado, his face sweet and open and full of pleasure. And then the hardness clamped down again, and he looked away.

She sighed. So it was going to be that way, was it? Well, she could give as good as she got. Moving on into the kitchen, she plunked herself down on a stool at the counter and smiled at him. He was really going to love the babysitting plan.

It wasn't until he looked up from the albondigas soup he was stirring and saw her coming toward him through the café that he realized what a good thing it was that he hadn't had a nightgown to loan her. She looked utterly delicious in his shirt, cute and cuddly and seductive as all hell. Her legs looked long and smooth, and her breasts...

Good Lord, why did she have to have breasts, too? Wasn't a pretty face and a sexy voice bad enough?

He quickly turned his attention back to preparing for lunch, turning from the soup to the cutting board, and grunted an answer to her greeting, but his mind was still full of the picture he'd just taken in.

"Excuse my casual attire," she murmured, obviously aware of the effect she was having on him.

Excuse it? How the hell was he going to excuse it? He hardly dared look at it. But no matter how much attention he tried to pay to cutting up tomatoes for salsa, the picture that had seared into his mind remained.

She looked just like one of those shirt ads, or a scene from a movie where the hero and heroine wake up in a penthouse suite overlooking Manhattan, looking as though they'd made love all night. Her eyes were just a little bit sleepy, her body just a little bit gorgeous. The cleavage between her breasts showed where the crisp cotton shirt was buttoned low, and her hair was piled on top of her head, wisps flying out around her face. Any man who found someone like this in his bed in the morning...

Whoa. Hold on. She's Reed's sister, he told himself in grim silence, staring hard at an onion he was about to eviscerate. "No lust allowed."

"You don't really do this for a living, do you?" she was asking.

It took effort not to look up and meet her eyes, but he managed it. "What? Cook?"

She nodded. "I'm sure you do it very well," she hastened to add. "But it just doesn't seem ..."

"No," he said shortly, taking a very shiny, sharp knife and making mince meat of the cilantro, just as he'd done to the onion, getting satisfaction out of every crushing blow. Hah. Die, small green things.

"I'm a landscape architect," he said aloud. "I have my own firm in San Diego."

"Really?" She leaned forward, enjoying watching him work, her chin in her hand. "I live in San Diego, too, in La Jolla."

"Do you?" He stabbed a ripe tomato right through the heart and watched it bleed. He wasn't always so rough with the vegetables, but he had to get rid of his frustrations somehow.

"Yes." She went on breezily, not seeming to notice the mayhem going on right under her nose. "Right now I'm staying at my parents' summer home there."

The summer home that jutted out from the cliff, over-looking the waves. He'd seen it. The place was about as far from his middle-class residential section as earth was from the mountains of the moon. La Jolla, indeed. He took a fork and mashed the salsa as though it were an enemy he'd been chasing for a long, long time.

She quit trying to make conversation, which was even worse. He went on smashing food while she sat and stared at him, and the silence grew as heavy as a wet blanket draped between them. Finally he couldn't stand it any longer, and he looked up, meeting her gaze, disconcerted to find her eyes full of amusement. What the hell did she think she was laughing at?

"Would you like some coffee?" he asked gruffly.

She nodded, her tongue moistening her lips as she tried to hold back a smile. "I would love some. Thanks."

He poured it without looking at her again.

"Thank you," she said softly, but he didn't answer.

She took the cup in her hands and sniffed the aroma with sensual pleasure. Glancing up, he saw the look on her face and felt his stomach muscles contract, and everything be-low it followed suit. His fingers tightened around the knife. He needed something else to attack, but slashing tortillas to ribbons might strike her as a little strange.

"So you come down every summer to help your grand-parents out?" she asked, seemingly as tired of the silence as he was.

"If I didn't come," he said, throwing scraps into the paper liner of the garbage pail—throwing them hard—"they wouldn't take a vacation. There's really no one else who could run it for them this way."

"What a nice thing to do," she noted softly.

He glanced at her as he washed off the cutting board with hot, hot water. "I enjoy it. I do it as much to get away for a while as anything else. It's not just to help them."

She laughed. "Oh. Sorry if I implied you might actually have a soft spot."

Sure he had a soft spot. Couldn't she see it? It was right on the top of his head.

But enough of this. He turned and looked her full in the face, leaning both hands on the counter before her. He couldn't take much more of this pussyfooting around. He didn't like being teased. Maybe she didn't know she was teasing him. Maybe she was just chatty. Well, if she wanted conversation, he would give it to her.

"You want to talk?" he said evenly. "Okay. Let's talk about what you're doing here in Puerto Vallarta. That is, if you've had time to straighten things out in your mind."

He held her gaze with his own and something sparked in the shimmering blue of her eyes. For a moment he thought she was going to snap back at him. But she held her anger in check this time. Slowly she nodded.

"Okay, David," she said calmly. "I guess it's time I told you everything."

He waited, face hard and expressionless. She bit her lip and avoided his eyes for a moment.

"Have you ever heard of Armand Alexiakis?" she asked at last.

He frowned. "Wasn't that the name of the Greek millionaire you married?"

"You knew about that?"

"Reed said something about it once."

She looked down at her hands. "Yes. Well, I did marry him."

He knew that. Hell, there were two kids sleeping upstairs to prove it.

"Was he the one you were with on the yacht?" She nodded and he looked away. The woman had a husband. That made the way he was feeling about her even worse. "So... what happened? You had a fight?"

She took a deep breath and went on. "Well, we're not married anymore. But he was the one I was with."

"Really?" He felt as though all the air had suddenly been sucked out of him, like a bad balloon. It took effort just to stay where he was and face her. No longer married. What do you know?

"I divorced him almost three years ago," she said, and he looked up in time to catch the bleak look on her face. "But he is the children's father."

David nodded. Reed had mentioned his sister's disastrous marriage. Normally, he shied away from divorced women. They were so often bitter, or they wanted to prove they were still desirable and came on too strong. But Shelley... hell, what was he thinking of? Divorced or not, she was poison. He had to remember that. Swallowing hard, he listened to what she was saying.

"And when he invited us down to visit him here, I thought it would be a good chance for Jill and Chris to get to know him. They hadn't seen him for years."

"And now he wants you back," David guessed. It only seemed logical.

She hesitated. "Yes. In a way."

"And you don't want to stay with him."

"Exactly."

He nodded slowly. "Was he trying to force you to stay?"

"Yes. He . . . he was getting obsessed with it. He frightened me."

You could hardly blame the guy for getting uptight about the situation. Still, he had no right to scare her.

"Well, we'll get the three of you on a plane this afternoon, and you won't have to worry about him anymore. I assume you have security at your house in La Jolla?"

"Of course. But you see—he'll probably be watching the airports. And the banks. I'm going to need a disguise."

"What?" He looked at her again, wondering if there was something about her he hadn't noticed before—like a screw loose.

She saw the skepticism in his eyes, and she frowned. "I'm serious, David. I tried to leave day before yesterday, and he threatened me. I don't dare risk seeing him again." She paused and looked at him earnestly. "Don't you see?" she asked desperately. "If he got hold of the children, he might not give them back. He could . . . blackmail me."

David nodded slowly, his nerves sizzling from the sound of her low, husky voice. Okay, he could buy that. He'd heard of things like that before. Rejected husband grabs kids to make ex-wife reconsider. Maybe she was right to be careful.

"That's why I need you to baby-sit for me," she said, watching his eyes for his reaction.

The eyes widened in horror. "Baby-sit?" Hadn't he heard this one before? "Oh, no. I'm not really good with kids. I tell you what. I know plenty of girls in this neighborhood who would . . ."

She was shaking her head emphatically. "No. You're the only one I can trust, David. That's why I came to you. Armand will have his men out all over the place." She leaned forward. "It won't be for long. I just have to go to the bank and arrange for funds to be transferred so I can get new airline tickets.''

Baby-sitting. He felt sulky. He didn't want to do it. "What happened to the old ones?"

"Armand has them. I couldn't very well ask for them back as I was slipping out the back way. I shouldn't be too long at the bank, but I can't take the kids with me. Armand's men would spot us for sure. I need some clothes, something that looks local, and maybe a wig...."

He shook his head. Caution was one thing, but she was really going over the top with this one. "Shelley, are you sure you aren't carrying this a little far? I mean, the man can't be everywhere."

Her eyes were clear. She didn't look like a nut case. "No, but his men can. They'll search all of Puerto Vallarta for us. Believe me, David, I know him."

She stared at him hard, her eyes wide with candor. He had no doubt she believed every word she said. Still, it just seemed a bit too melodramatic to him.

"I know he'll be watching every place he can think of, every place he thinks I might visit," she said again. "That's why I can't take the children with me. They'd be a dead giveaway."

His mouth twisted. He was going to have to baby-sit, that was clear. Still, he thought the whole thing was a little ridiculous.

"Should we expect spies coming in here, too?" he asked, half joking.

"Oh, no, I don't think so," she replied with a fleeting smile. "It would take him a while before he'd suspect I was in this part of town. When we were together, our life-style was pretty extreme and he got the idea I couldn't live any other way. I'm sure he'll be concentrating on the four-star hotels.''

Well, that was really laying it on the line. His head went back at her words, but she didn't notice the reaction in his eyes. Still, what was he so upset about? She was only stating the obvious. They came from different worlds. And she was only visiting in this one. And not for long. The sooner she left and his pulse got back to normal, the better.

"Okay," he said briefly. "I'll get some stuff you can use for a disguise. And I'll watch your kids for you. You can take my car."

"Thanks." Her smile seemed to shimmer at him and he turned away quickly, going back to cooking to save his soul.

But she didn't take the hint. Instead of leaving the room, she slipped down off the stool and came around to where he couldn't avoid her.

"David," she challenged him, her hands on her hips. "Why don't you like me?"

He looked up, his dark eyes impenetrable. She was close and lovely. All he had to do was reach out his hand and . . . He pulled himself back. "Who said I didn't like you?" he asked huskily.

She shook her head, studying him, but not quite sure. "Your eyes say it every time you look at me."

He winced and laughed shortly, turning away from her scrutiny. "Then my eyes are lying," he said, reaching for a large jelly roll pan.

He missed it. It fell and they both bent to retrieve it, coming up, each holding one end.

"I want to help you," she said, not letting go. "What can I do?"

Put on a snowsuit, die your hair green, get an ugly case of chicken pox, and lose that voice. Or just leave town. Nothing else was going to help at all.

"You don't need to do anything," he said aloud, still holding his end of the pan.

"Yes I do. You've given us shelter, and I have to pay you back somehow. Let me help you get things ready."

She was going to hold on to the pan until he cried uncle, that was obvious. He shrugged. "All right."

She let go of the pan, and he turned around to set it on the counter and begin setting chili-wrapped cheese wedges in straight lines. "You can help fix these chilies."

"Okay." She hovered close, ready for whatever he told her to do, but making a rueful face. "There's only one problem. I don't know how to cook."

He stared at her, chilies suspended in midair. "You don't know how to cook? How could you get to this stage of life and not know how to cook?"

She made a face that was so adorable he had to swallow hard to keep from grabbing her with the chili still in his hands. "I've never had to know how. There's always been someone to do it for me."

She said it so simply, with no regret, no embarrassment. A life with servants waiting on you hand and foot—was this for real? And yet he knew it was. He'd seen it himself when he'd visited the Brittman home in the Hamptons.

He tossed the chili down in the pan, frowning. "I would think that simple curiosity would have compelled you to learn how to cook something." He knew he sounded a bit grumpy, but why not? That was the rich for you. Living off the work of others. Looking down their noses at people who actually knew what they were doing. Making love in the afternoon...

Damn, why couldn't he get his mind off romance?

"I did cook fudge once, with some girlfriends." She looked rather wistful. "That was a long time ago."

"Fudge." He shook his head, narrowing his eyes. She would look better in whipped cream. A little smeared here, a little smeared there . . . He coughed and blinked, hard, focusing his mind.

"Well, I'll tell you, you come here and take this whisk to these eggs as though it were fudge, okay?" He handed her a bowl into which he'd broken almost a dozen eggs.

"Okay." She took it gingerly. "Like this?" She began to run the whisk awkwardly through the eggs.

Not exactly, but she would surely get it as she went along. "Uh, sort of." He helped her hold the whisk at a better angle, then drew back quickly, not wanting to touch her.

She began to beat, looking clumsy but willing.

"How did you learn to cook?" she asked as he began tossing tomatoes into a large pot over a medium flame on the stove.

"It was a matter of survival. I spent a lot of time being the only one at home when I was a kid. If I wanted to eat, I had to cook."

"Really?" She smiled at him. "Where did you grow up?"

He turned away from her, frowning. How did they get on the subject of his background? It wasn't something he normally liked to talk about. "Los Angeles, mostly."

"Mostly?"

Women were never satisfied with short answers. "Los Angeles with my father. Kansas City with my mother. And summers I came down here with my grandparents."

"You did a lot of traveling."

True. And not first class, either. But then, what would she know about economy night flights and taking the bus to save a few dollars? She didn't even know how to cook.

He looked over to see how she was doing and found she'd done a mediocre job beating the eggs. They were going to need more elbow grease. But she looked tired, so he shifted her to wrapping chilies around strips of cheese while he finished mixing together the tomato sauce.

"Oh, do I need an apron?" she asked suddenly.

He glanced at the shirt she was wearing. "No," he said quickly. Despite everything, he couldn't stand the thought of all those lovely curves being hidden behind an apron. She was backlit right now, from the morning sunlight coming in the windows. He could barely see the rounded hips, the swaying breasts beneath the thin cotton cloth. Something caught in his throat, choking him for a moment, and then he looked away. But the image stayed with him. He'd never seen a woman before who turned him on so easily. Maybe if he stuck his head under the faucet and turned on the cold water...

She nodded, then looked up. "David," she asked with some chagrin. "You're going to have to help me out here. What exactly are we making?"

He looked at her and almost laughed aloud. She looked so damn appealing. But it was incredible—he'd never known anyone so sheltered from normal life.

"Right now we're working on the chilies rellenos for the lunch shift. I make a casserole of it instead of the individual chilies like we have at dinner. That way I can cut out a square and use it as a side dish for almost anything else."

"Chilies rellenos," she repeated, pronouncing it pretty well. "I've had that before. It's delicious."

She turned and started working on the eggs again, her lip caught by her teeth as she concentrated, but she was doing it all wrong. Her arm was at an awkward angle and she was splashing half the egg mixture out of the bowl. He smiled and put down the knife he was using, moving toward her.

"No, here. Like this."

As he reached across her to take the whisk, he got too close to her and the scent of her hair filled his head. For just a moment he thought he was seeing stars. From this angle he could see right down the front of the shirt she wore, see her high, firm breasts. They were so softly curved, with the dark, pointed nipples erect as though they'd been rubbing against the cloth. He looked away quickly, his heart pumping something into his veins that felt like liquid gold.

He was frozen, standing stock-still. She turned her face up toward his, so close, a look of wonder in her eyes. The temptation to kiss her was so strong, he wasn't sure he could resist. She had that look in her eyes, that look that said, well, maybe.... He knew she would let him kiss her, maybe even kiss him back.

But he also knew he wouldn't stop there. Once his lips had found hers and her warmth started to fill him, he would have to run his hands up under the shirt and touch her, to arouse her like she was arousing him. Desire was erupting inside him, a throbbing pressure in his body, a beating drum in his head, pushing and pounding and demanding he do something to get relief. He had to get away from her, but he couldn't breathe. It was like a dream where he had to run but he couldn't move.

But he could move, and finally he did, backing away, looking at Shelley as though she were an alien he'd suddenly discovered in his kitchen.

"Uh, listen, I can do this later," he muttered, reaching to take off his apron. "I'll run out and get those clothes for you to go to the bank."

"David?" she asked.

But he couldn't talk about this now. Turning, he didn't look back.

"I'll be gone about half an hour," he said as he went out the door. And once outside he leaned against the building and took in a huge swallow of air, filling his lungs as though he'd been suffocating.

"My God," he murmured as he fumbled with the key to his car. "I've got to get that woman out of here."

Four

Rosa was full of questions when David arrived at her house asking to borrow a wig and some clothes. He'd known she would be, but he didn't know what else he could do. She was the only one *he* could trust.

Despite her rampant curiosity, she gave him a bag full of clothes and other items, including a wig she hadn't worn for twenty years.

"It made me itch," she said. "But it looks so real, I couldn't throw it out."

"Thanks, Rosa." David said as he ran out the door, back to the woman who occupied his thoughts, and his home.

When he handed the wig to Shelley, it didn't look all that real on her head. Somehow the big black curls didn't go very well with her light skin and silver-blue eyes.

"I look like I belong in some jungle market with bananas on my head," she said, surveying herself in the mirror.

David grinned. "Well, you didn't want to look like Shelley Brittman. I think you've succeeded there."

She curled her lip and wrinkled her nose. "I didn't want to look like a character from a Saturday morning cartoon show, either. But I guess beggars can't be choosers."

The chartreuse capri pants and the huge polyester blouse with a parrot printed across it, combined with the wig, worked to create an image very different from what Shelley normally looked like, but they hardly looked cartoony. In fact, if anything, they served to help her fit in with the bright colors natives wore, as well as tourists who traveled into town.

And the clothes did more than that. They helped David feel more comfortable with her.

"Gee, I really wish I'd had these when I was on the yacht," Shelley quipped, looking at herself in the full-length mirror in his room. "Just the thing for an afternoon on the high seas."

David nodded, marveling that a wig and some tacky clothes could make her look so much less threatening to his seemingly fragile state of mind. "It might have been appropriate for Carnival in Rio," he suggested.

She laughed and spun around to face him. "Or trick or treat almost anywhere in the world. If only Armand could see me now, he might just give up any hopes of getting me to cruise the coast with him."

"Was that what he was planning?"

She nodded. "A week here, and then on down to South America. He wanted us to spend six weeks together. He actually used the excuse of Valentine's Day coming up as an incentive."

"Ah, the old Valentine's Day ploy."

Suddenly they were grinning at each other like old friends.

"Has someone used it on you in the past?" she asked him.

He nodded, looking morose. "Not quite the way your ex-husband used it on you, but it was almost as disastrous. Two girls once kidnapped me, dressed me in a cupid's costume, and forced me to sell my favors in a kissing booth at a Valentine's Day fair."

She laughed. "The horror of it all. That must have been really hard for you, considering how you feel about kissing."

His eyebrows rose. "Who said I didn't like kissing?" And then he remembered what had happened in the kitchen just before he'd left to get the clothes. She'd known what he'd been feeling, how much he'd wanted to take her in his arms. She probably thought he was the biggest fool she'd ever known.

But she wasn't laughing at him. Instead she was studying him, her head to the side. "I didn't say you didn't like kissing," she said solemnly. "It's just that you're not the kissy-huggy sort. You're more the dark, brooding type, aren't you?"

He laughed, shaking his head. "No, Shelley, I'm not. I think you've got me pegged all wrong."

With her lower lip stuck out in thought, she studied him for a moment more, shaking her head. "I'll get you figured out yet," she said softly, and then she turned back to the mirror. "But in the meantime, I've got to get this right. I do look completely different, but I'm not sure it's enough." She frowned into the reflection. "My face still shows. Maybe some heavy makeup..."

"Here," David offered, handing her a pair of sunglasses Rosa had thrown into the bag.

She put them on and shook her head.

"Where did you have to go to get these, nineteen fifty-five?"

Old-fashioned though they were, they did the trick. She looked like a totally different person.

"A totally ridiculous person," she contended, and David had to admit she was right. It was sort of sad to see the tantalizing reality fade away and this tacky fiction take its place. But there were compensations. His risk of a sudden heart attack had gone way down, and he began to feel more like his normal self again.

Jill laughed when she saw her mother dressed up like someone else, but Chris's lower lip began to tremble, and Shelley had to sit and hold him for a few minutes until he got used to the idea.

"You two are going to stay with David," she told them. "He's going to take care of you for a couple of hours." The two children turned to stare at him, and he felt as nakedly vulnerable as a man on trial for murder.

"We'll have fun," he claimed with false heartiness. "We'll..." Words failed him. What did kids like to do, anyway?

Shelley jumped in to help him out, laughing at him at the same time. "Why don't you two go on down to the café while David finishes getting things ready? Chris, you can bring your coloring book. And Jill you can work on your journal."

"Good idea," he chimed in. "Just what I was thinking."

She grinned at him and for once, he smiled back. It was easier to smile when he couldn't see her blue eyes. The sunglasses were so much less intimidating.

He gave her his keys and walked out to the car with her to show her the fundamentals of the controls. She sat in the driver's seat while he demonstrated where the gears sat and which knob controlled the turn signal.

When he finally reached for the door, about to let her go, she stopped him with a hand on his arm.

"David, why is it you're being so friendly all of a sudden?" she asked softly.

He knew why, but he certainly wasn't going to discuss it with her. "Why is it you want to analyze me all the time?" he countered, getting out of the car. "Good luck at the bank." He leaned down and smiled at her. "And don't take too long. If those kids have me gagged and tied to a chair, I'll be the one in need of rescuing."

She smiled and drove off. He turned back toward the café where his two charges were waiting for the baby-sitting to begin. At least, they were supposed to be waiting. When he stepped back into the café, he came-face-to-face with what handling children was really all about. Complete chaos.

Being of a curious state of mind and age, Chris had opened the back door to the alley—just to see what was behind it—and six alley cats streaked in, jumping on counters, knocking over the trash, fighting over the fish scraps in the sink. Jill had tried to pet one and had been scratched across the nose. She was in a heap on the floor, sobbing her heart out, more out of hurt feelings than pain. Chris was jumping up and down, yelling, "Go, cats, go!"

David didn't waste time going into shock, though that course of action was tempting to him. It took a few minutes to restore order, eject the cats and get Jill comforted and settled back down with her notebook. Chris, however, was not about to be consigned to the coloring book. He wanted to follow David's every move and ended up sitting on the counter where he could watch most everything and not get into too much.

But once his body was stilled, his mouth was free to go into overdrive, and the questions began. They were simple at first. Nothing overly complicated. But there were so many of them, and they just kept coming, no matter what David did or said. Was he really supposed to answer them all? And how was he supposed to keep his sanity?

"If there are hundreds of people on buses," he asked, his little face furled in concentration on this compelling subject, "how come they don't fly out when the bus goes around a corner?"

Whoa. David shook his head as he continued cutting halibut into filets for the midday meal. That was a toughie. It was also something of a non sequitur, but what the heck. He was just a little kid. He just didn't know.

"They're sitting in their seats," David explained calmly. "Why would they fly out?"

Chris blinked. "Birds do. I saw a bird fly out once."

David's smile was patient. "Birds are supposed to fly."

Chris nodded and looked pleased. "I bet I could fly. I had a dream, once."

"About flying?"

"No. 'Bout my tricycle. It has purple pedals. And a horn. I like to blow my horn. I race my tricycle and blow my horn all the time." He kicked his feet against the counter, looking more content than ever. "Could you come to my house and see me ride my tricycle?"

The kid was throwing him. First the questions which didn't make any sense, then the jumping from one subject to another. David was beginning to feel his shoulders tense up, and that meant he was losing it. He forced himself to remain calm.

"I'd like to come to your house and see you ride someday," he said carefully.

"When?" the boy demanded, waiting for an answer.

"Well, we'll have to work that out with your mother."

"How about next Sunday? Mama says we'll be home by Sunday. Could you come Sunday?"

"Maybe. We'll have to see."

"Okay. Are you a cowboy?"

David frowned, getting dizzy. "No, not really."

"Then how come you wear cowboy boots?"

David's shoulders felt as though they'd been encased in cement. He was going to have to count to ten before he dared answer the last one. "Because I like them," he said at last, trying to smile.

"And how come you wear a cowboy hat?"

This time he couldn't keep the brusqueness out of his voice. "To keep the sun off my head," he snapped, beginning to feel desperate.

But Chris didn't notice a thing. "How come you have to cook this food?" he went on blithely.

David's fingers tightened on the edge of the counter. "Because people are going to be coming to buy it."

Chris's eyes were wide and innocent of all malice. "How come?"

David was working hard at controlling himself now. He spoke slowly and with effort. "Because they'll be hungry."

"How come?"

The glass he'd been moving slipped out of his hand and shattered on the tiled floor, and David looked at it gratefully. "No more questions for a while, Chris," he said with relief. "I've got to clean up this mess."

"Okay," the boy said, so cheerfully cooperative it made David feel guilty.

As soon as he finished cleaning up the broken glass, he smiled at Chris. "Hey, how's that coloring coming?" he asked him.

"How come you don't have a TV?" Chris asked, ignoring David's question and launching right into one of his own.

David blinked. The questions were starting up again, and he didn't know how long he could take it. "I don't know. I guess my grandmother took her portable with her."

He looked at the boy. Well, here was the problem. He was letting the kid dictate the agenda here. If he took the initiative and guided the conversation, they might be able to handle something that didn't make him want to climb walls.

"You wouldn't want to watch TV here, anyway. All the programs are in Spanish," he said, trying to think of a direction to go in.

"I know Spanish," said Chris, providing one on his own.

"You do?" This was better. He grinned at the kid. "What do you know in Spanish?"

Chris's face contorted with effort and he yelled out, "*¡Sí!*" at the top of his lungs.

David laughed. "That's a good Spanish word. You want to learn something else in Spanish?"

Chris nodded, his eyes wide.

"Okay. Say this, *muchas gracias*. That means thank you."

"Moossh graassus."

"*Muchas gracias.*"

"Muchas grassssus."

"Good. Now say this, *buenos dias*. That means good morning. *Buenos dias*."

Chris frowned but his lips didn't seem to want to try it. Suddenly his face lit up. "I know another Spanish saying," he said proudly, and repeated a four-letter word that was not very polite.

David swallowed hard. "Uh, no, Chris. That's not a good Spanish word. And if you use it again, your mom will wash your mouth out with soap." He frowned. That desperate feeling was threatening again. What did he know about kids and how to respond to them? What if he were scarring this one for life? "Who taught that to you, anyway?" he asked in exasperation.

Chris shrugged.

"Well, for Pete's sake, don't go telling your mother you learned it from me."

"The men on the boat taught it to him," Jill chimed in from the table. "I told Mama and she told them to quit it."

David turned and smiled at her. He'd been ignoring the girl. Of course, the boy was so demanding of attention, and she was so quiet, that probably happened to her a lot. He decided to make an effort at drawing her out a little.

Sauntering over to her table, he flopped down into a chair. "What have you got there?" he asked, gesturing toward her notebook.

"My journal." Jill looked at him owlishly over the top of the notebook. "I keep track of things in here."

She was cute. He could see the potential for a woman very much like her mother inside her. "Oh, yeah? What sort of things?"

"Lists. And things about people."

"People?" It seemed a strange preoccupation for such a young girl.

She nodded, watching him. "I have pages for people."

"What sort of people?" he asked, expecting to hear about her little friends back home.

"The people mama goes out with," she told him serenely.

Okay, now he was interested. He leaned forward, his chin in his hands and smiled at her. "You mean, men?"

She nodded.

He eyed the notebook the notebook. "No kidding. Does your mother . . . ah . . . go out with a lot of men?"

Jill shook her head. "No. We're trying to make her."

He stared at the little girl, not sure whether to smile or suppress it. She was undoubtedly the oddest girl he'd ever known. But then, how many little girls did he know? Maybe they were all like this these days.

"You're trying to make her go out with a lot of men?" he repeated, just wanting to get it straight.

Jill nodded. "We wanna get a daddy."

Ah-hah. So that was it. But wait. Wasn't there a catch? "I . . . I thought you had a daddy."

Jill shook her head, completely matter-of-fact about it. "We don't like him. We want somebody we like."

Just as candid as her mother. He shook his head. He'd never known a pair of women like this before.

Jill was still staring at him. She laid the notebook down on the table, open to a page that had a lot of writing on it. "Want to see?" she asked.

David drew himself up. Of course not. That would be totally classless. Not to mention snoopy and insulting.

"Uh . . ."

"Here."

She put the book in front of him, wide open. It wasn't as though he'd asked to see it. He leaned forward, completely absorbed.

"This page is all about Cubby Van Brinkster. See, I wrote down his birthday and where he was born and what he looks like. And then I say things about him. And I ask Chris what he thinks, and I put down what he says, too. 'Cuz it would be his father, too."

"Very sporting of you," David murmured, looking the page over. Cubby was tall and blond and very athletic, it seemed. La Crosse, tennis, polo, race horses. Jill had tried to draw a picture but her drawing ability left a lot to be desired at this stage and it wasn't very revealing.

"If she would marry Cubby Van Brinkster, he would be a good dad," Jill said.

David drew back, not sure he wanted to hear this. "Would he?"

She nodded. "Yeah. He likes to play with kids. And every time he comes over he brings us new stuffed animals. One time he brought us a tent and we put it up in the living room and pretended we were camping out." She giggled, remembering.

David made a wry face. Now there was a boy who was working on the assumption that the way to Shelley's heart was through her children. And maybe he was right. She sure did care about those kids.

"He sounds like a pretty good guy. What does he do for a living?"

"I don't know." She frowned, thinking hard. "But maybe he works in a circus. Mama said once that he's a clown."

David felt a grin spreading across his face. "Ah. I see." So much for Cubby. He turned the page.

"This is Jim Stockman. He works in a bank. He brings Mama big presents. He brought her a car once. She made him take it back."

A rich guy, no doubt. "Tall," the journal noted. "Brown hair. Ugly brown suits."

"He comes and surprises Mama," Jill went on. "Then he always says, 'Couldn't the kids go and stay over at someone's house tonight?'"

David almost hated himself for what he asked next. "And what does Mama say to that?" he asked, careful to keep his eyes lowered.

Jill's nose could scrape the sky just like her mother's. "She says, 'Nope. My kids come first.'"

David felt his shoulders relax. "Good for Mama," he said softly. Right. So much for gentleman Jim and his fancy presents. He turned the page.

"Oh, that's Kyle Tanner. He drives race cars. He took Mama to France and we didn't like it 'cuz we had to stay with Grandma and she always has parties."

Took her to France. David felt a coldness encasing his heart. Kyle might be the one to watch. Cubby was obviously a front runner with the kids, but Kyle was the one who got her to take a trip with him.

All of this was none of his business, of course. A woman as beautiful as Shelley was bound to have male suitors all over the place. And naturally she would like some of them, like them enough to...

Okay, what was happening inside him now was stupid. He had no right to be jealous. There was nothing to be jealous of. She wasn't his. He wasn't even one of Jill's candidates. Shelley wasn't even going to be here longer than a few more hours. Then she would be gone and he would never see her again. Never see her again.... Why did that set up an ache in his gut?

"How do you and Chris like this Tanner fellow?"

Jill shrugged. "I don't know. We don't ever get to see him. We didn't go to France."

Good answer. Logical. Straight forward. "I see." He'd had enough of Kyle. It was time to turn the page.

And that was where the shock came in. Armand Alexiakis was the name at the top of the sheet.

He glanced at her sideways. "That's your father, isn't it?"

She nodded but didn't make any comment. But she didn't have to. He could read the comments for himself. The first notations were written in a steady hand in blue ink and probably made just before they'd come down to Mexico. "My real daddy. Handsome. Rich. Has a boat."

Then, in different ink and more ragged writing, "Mean, yells a lot, hates kids, made Mama cry."

He looked up and met Jill's eyes. They were steady and clear. "I don't like him," she said softly. "Is that bad?"

She was asking him? Well, why not? He was a child of divorce himself. He knew the pain of separation, trying to please two different parents at the same time, always feeling guilty that you couldn't please either of them enough—never enough to get them back together again.

But he'd loved both his parents. How much worse it must be if you didn't love one of them. That must cut the supports right out from under a kid. Someone should talk to Jill about what she was feeling.

But how could he talk about things like this with a kid? He looked away and was saved from having to answer as Rosa came hurrying through the door.

"Rosa," he said, surprised. "Is it already…?" He looked at his watch and groaned. The two hours had gone by much more quickly than he would have thought. "Ten minutes to opening and I'm not ready." He rose from the seat and turned to greet the older woman.

"*Hola,*" Rosa said, plunking her things down on the table where Jill was sitting. "Who is this?"

"This is Jill. She's visiting, along with her brother." David turned to include Chris and found only empty air. The counter was bare. The coloring book sat unused. "Hey. Where's Chris?"

Jill shrugged. David swore under his breath and raced upstairs, shouting for the boy as he ran.

Rosa watched it all with interest, then turned and eyed the girl. "Where's your mama, *niña?*"

Jill looked up, eyes clear and bright. "She's gone to get money for us at the bank. She had to dress up in funny clothes. She'll be back soon."

Rosa's eyebrows rose. "Did she wear a wig, too?" she asked, her voice shaking.

Jill nodded. "And funny glasses."

"To go to the bank and get money?" Rosa asked. A look of horror spread across her face. She started to say more, but before she had a chance to ask another question, David came running back down the stairs. "He's not up there. He must have slipped out. That kid—" He started for the door, then looked back. "Hey, Rosa, will you keep your eye on Jill? I've got to find Chris."

Rosa nodded, frowning, but he didn't wait to hear her answer. He was out the door and gone. Rosa turned back to the little girl.

"Is your mama an old friend of David's?" she asked worriedly.

Jill shook her head. "We just came last night. He said we could stay here." She leaned closer to Rosa and whispered conspiratorially. "We're running away."

Rosa gave a cry and threw up her hands and let out a string of Spanish that Jill didn't understand. When David reappeared, a recalcitrant Chris in tow, she followed him, talking so fast he couldn't get a word in edgewise.

Jill watched, fascinated, wondering what the woman was saying. But then David turned, laughing, and took the woman into his arms, hugging her with warm affection, patting her back, calming her down.

"Cool it, Rosa," he said at last. "I'm not getting involved in bank holdups. I swear to God. Quiet down and I'll explain it all to you."

Jill watched as he did just that. The woman wiped tears from her eyes and said things in Spanish. David laughed and looked at her with love, and Jill opened up her notebook to a fresh page. "David Coronado," she wrote at the top of the sheet. "Very handsome," she added. And then she waited, pen poised, for more of him to be revealed.

Five

David didn't have time to start worrying about Shelley until the noon rush had subsided a bit. That was when it hit him. She wasn't back. How long did it take to get money from a bank?

Rosa was being great with the kids, now that she'd calmed down and accepted the true state of affairs. Instead of consigning Jill and Chris to the bedroom upstairs, she gave them jobs to do, helping her take orders and serve the food, and the customers were enchanted by the tiny new staff. Most of them had known David for years and were as much friends as customers. He got a lot of teasing about being a baby-sitting bachelor, and the women cooed over the kids. All in all, it worked out well.

But Shelley wasn't back. It beat like a drum behind everything he did. *Shelley wasn't back.*

It was almost two o'clock—afternoon closing time—and the kids were getting cranky.

"I'll put them down for a nap," Rosa offered, and as there were only a few customers left in the café, David nodded.

The bell on the front door rang just as they reached the stairs. David looked up. A dark man in a light suit was entering, and every nerve in David's body pulsed. This was no local. This wasn't even a tourist. The moment he saw the man, David knew exactly what he wanted.

The man didn't sit at a table. He didn't slide onto a stool at the counter, either. He came right back into the kitchen and nodded to David as though he had been there before, his eyes cold and cunning.

"I'm looking for someone," he said shortly in Spanish, pulling out a picture. "Have you seen this woman, or these kids?"

David didn't give the picture more than a quick glance, then shook his head. "Never seen them before in my life," he lied.

The man didn't seem surprised, or even very interested. He nodded, put the picture away, and pulled out a card. "If you think you see them or have any information about them, call this number. There'll be a reward for somebody in this."

David took the card he held out, though every instinct in his body was crying out for him to do violence to this man instead. "Okay," he managed to say, keeping his voice steady. "I'll keep it in mind."

The man turned to go and suddenly a shrieking giggle of hilarity split the air and Jill's voice rang out in obvious American English. "Stop tickling!"

David froze with dread. If this were one of the men who had known the kids on the yacht, he might recognize the voice. At the very least, he had to know there was a North American kid upstairs. The man stopped and looked up toward where the voice had come from, and David began judging the distance to the nearest knife and just how long it would take him to reach it.

"My kids," he said quickly, in English this time, letting the man hear his own American accent. "Can't keep 'em quiet."

The man looked at him, his eyes hard. Then he nodded curtly. "That's why I don't have any of the little jerks myself," he said, and turned to leave the kitchen area.

David reached for the knife and held it in his hand, his nerves steady, adrenaline pumping through his body. His gaze never left the man. If he stopped and showed that picture to any one of the customers lingering over coffee, they would instantly recognize the kids. And then David would have to do something extreme.

But the man didn't stop, and in another moment, he'd passed through the café and was gone.

David let all the air out of his lungs in a rush. Suddenly he had new respect for Shelley's paranoia. Her ex-husband really was searching the town for her, and using some hardened characters to do it. Unbelievable.

But where the hell was she? He wanted to go out and look for her, but he couldn't leave the kids. He did go ahead and close the café early, hoping Rosa would stay with the children while he went out and scoured the banks, but she couldn't stay. She had a dentist's appointment she'd been waiting for all month, and she wailed and beat her breast and then promised to be back just as soon as possible so that he could go.

"I'll call as soon as I get back from the dentist and see if you still need me," she said. "Then I'll watch them all the rest of the afternoon, if need be."

He had to be satisfied with that. He went upstairs and watched the children sleep, pacing restlessly. If anything had happened to Shelley—if Armand had grabbed her—

It rang inside him. If Armand had grabbed her, he would get her back. No matter what he had to do, that bastard wasn't going to hurt her again.

He didn't know what the man had done, but he could read the signs. Shelley was strong and proud, but something had hurt her. A person didn't get that haunted look for no reason.

He slumped into a chair and stared at the two blond heads on the pillows. All he wanted to do was rush out and protect Shelley. Instead, here he was, baby-sitting. Next thing you know, he'd be reading romances.

He must have dozed, because suddenly she was there, coming in across the room. She'd pulled off the wig, and her blond hair was floating around her shoulders again. For just a second he thought he was dreaming, but then he came fully awake and pulled himself to his feet.

"What is it?" he said. "What happened?"

He could see in her eyes that something was wrong.

She put her finger to her lips and nodded toward where the children were sleeping, then led the way out onto the landing where she sank down onto his couch. Reaching back, she swept the hair up from her neck and leaned her head back, eyes closed. He moved beside her, sitting gingerly on the edge of the cushion, wary of getting too close. She was dangerous again. He had to be careful.

She opened her eyes and smiled at him. "Well, David, it seems that as far as Mexico is concerned, I don't exist."

He frowned. "What are you talking about?"

"I told you I'd called Reed and had him wire money. I went to every bank in town. I talked to bank vice presidents by the score. Most of them thought I was a nut case, thanks to the zany attire. The others were very sorry, but they just couldn't do anything at all for me until I provide the proper identification.''

David stared at her, not understanding. "They wouldn't take your California driver's license... your tourist card...?"

She shook her head. "David, didn't I tell you? Armand has my purse and all my papers in his safe. I don't have anything I can use to prove who I am.'' That hardly seemed credible. There had to be some way.

"There's not a branch of your personal bank here in town?"

She shook her head. "There's a branch of the bank my father uses, and they were very nice, but they can't do anything for me until I either provide ID, or get my father to call.''

He snapped his fingers. "The consular agency. There's one right here in town. They'll help you.''

She raised an eyebrow. "Will they? Not if Armand has anything to say about it. He's got someone inside the office.''

David looked skeptical. He had learned to respect this Armand's villainy a little more than before, but this seemed ludicrous. "How do you know that?''

She flattened her hands against the polyester pants. "He told me so when I tried to leave the other day.''

David shook his head. "I don't believe it. He was bluffing.''

She shrugged, her eyes shadowed by a hopelessness he hadn't seen there before. "Maybe so. But I can't afford to take a chance.''

He wanted to reach for her, take her hand. "We'll go to the consulate in Mazatlan,'' he offered.

She sighed, pushing her hair back with a weary gesture. "No, it's much too far. Besides, Armand will probably have men watching it."

For once he didn't scoff at her supposition. He knew better, now. "Someone came by here about an hour ago."

Her eyes widened and she sat up straighter. "Here? What did he look like? What did he say? Did he mention Armand?"

He told her briefly. "I guess you're right. Your ex-husband is serious about finding you and the kids."

"Oh, he's serious all right. He made that very clear." Her eyes clouded and she looked into the distance. "I just don't understand why."

David could understand it. All anyone had to do was look at her. "He wants you back," he said huskily, looking away so she wouldn't be able to read the way he felt in his eyes. "What's to understand?"

She smiled at him and reached out, taking his hand in her own. "That's very sweet," she said softly, "but not quite accurate."

Sweet. There was nothing sweet about what he was feeling toward her. Her touch ignited something inside him and he had a hard time keeping his breathing even. He couldn't answer. His gaze was riveted to her hand, her fingers laced with his, the nails pink and softly rounded. He felt suspended, somehow, as though he didn't need to breathe any longer, as though all he needed was her touch....

She was looking at their hands, too, enjoying the way his long, tapered fingers curled around her short ones. His hands were big and strong. She was glad he was muscular and solid. She almost felt safe with him.

Not that she really was, of course. It was all an illusion. She hadn't met a man yet you could really count on. Look at Armand. She'd actually thought she was in love with him once.

Still, it wasn't fair to paint David with the same brush. He'd been gruff and strangely aloof, but he'd also been kind and honest—and the sight of him dozing in the chair a few minutes ago, near her two little ones, had truly touched her.

She could talk to David. He was Reed's friend. That almost made him family, didn't it? Not that she talked to her family all that much. She tried to let her parents think everything was all right so they wouldn't worry, but she could be straight with David. So she turned and looked into his eyes and went on.

"I know he wasn't really interested in having me back for romantic reasons because of one very simple fact. He had his girlfriend on board."

She suddenly lowered her eyes again. Despite everything, that had been a blow. She didn't want Armand, she didn't love him, and she knew he didn't love her any longer. And yet, somehow, for him to pretend that he did and at the same time have the girl he really wanted on board, had been a humiliating insult. It wasn't logical, and yet—there it was.

David was frowning. Things weren't making sense to him. "Why would he do a stupid thing like that if he were trying to convince you he wanted you?"

She laughed, shaking her head. "Because he is a very arrogant man. He thinks he can have anything he wants. He wanted me back, but he wanted his girlfriend, too. So he brought her along. He's sure he knows better than anyone else. So he does arrogant things."

David was studying her eyes, searching them. The more he heard about this man, the more he hated him. "Why did you ever marry him?" he asked softly, truly puzzled and disturbed by that very act. She was so wonderful. How could she have thrown herself away on such a louse?

Her eyes darkened and she pulled her hand away. "That was long ago and far away," she said evasively. "Back to the problem at hand. I know what I'm going to have to do. I'll call my father. He'll come through for me. He always does." She made a face. "Which is precisely why I don't really want to call him," she murmured, more to herself than to him.

"He'll wire you the money?" But of course. Her father was rich and powerful. He could get anyone moving with a phone call. There really was no problem here. For a moment he'd thought she would be staying longer, and a part of him had turned traitor and he'd been glad. But that was just a pipe dream, anyway. She was going. Rich people always got what they wanted.

"Sure. Or get the bank to give me what I need." She sighed. "The only thing is, I didn't tell them I was coming down here, or that I was going to see Armand again. They're going to be upset, first that I did it, then that I didn't tell them I was doing it. Now I'll have to go through all the explanations and hear all the little lectures." She shrugged. "Oh, well. Nothing comes free, does it?"

She pulled herself up off the couch and looked down at the capris, the polyester blouse with the bizarre parrot. This really wasn't her. She had to regroup and begin to feel like herself again.

"Listen, I have to change out of these clothes. Do you have anything at all that I could wear?"

He rose to face her. "I don't think you'd fit into any of my slacks or jeans," he noted, glancing down at her slender figure. "But I might have a cotton sweater or a T-shirt you could wear."

He hesitated. No, he did not want to go in with her and start rummaging through clothes, watching her try things on. Down that road lay disaster. "Why don't you just go

ahead and choose anything you like? I've got to go down
and get things cleaned up for the dinner hour.''

She thanked him and slipped back into the room where
her children slept. He turned and walked down the stairs.

But the image of her stayed with him. He could still feel
her warm hand in his. The line of her cheek, the way her
eyes tilted at the corners, the curve of her mouth, all these
things affected him in ways he'd never been affected by a
woman before. More the way a beautiful strain of classical
music made him feel, reaching in to twist his heart with its
poignant beauty. That's what looking at Shelley did to him.
It twisted his heart.

He'd been captivated by her as he had never been by another woman in his life. Every masculine instinct he possessed told him to go after her, reach for her, woo her. And
at the same time, knowing what he did about her and her
background, he knew very well that giving in to that attraction would be like heading his car for the nearest cliff and
driving over it. She was out of his league—far, far out. He
would help her, but he would have to keep up his guard to
do it. The best thing he could do for his own peace of mind
was to stay as detached as possible.

Shelley looked down at her sleeping children and sighed.
It was always such a pleasure to look at them. Her heart
swelled inside her, she loved them so. They were her pride
and joy—and the proof that the last seven years of her life
hadn't been wasted. She would fight tooth and nail to keep
them. Armand must never, ever get his hands on them. Just
the thought of them having to live with that man made her
skin crawl.

When she thought about it, she realized that the last few
years had been a lull in her life. She'd been waiting for
something and hadn't realized it at the time. Now she knew

what it was. She'd needed to finish things off with Armand. She had to know if it was really over, or if he was still going to play a part in their lives. She'd been waiting for the shoe to drop.

Well, it had dropped with a thump that had rocked the boat, capsizing it. That was over. No more regrets—she was going to go on with her life. And to that end she was anxious to get back home.

But for that to happen, she was going to have to call her father. She made a face, thinking about that. She dreaded the conversation she was going to have to endure. She'd called him with too much bad news in the past. This made her feel like a kid again, that same old bubbleheaded, ditzy blonde everyone had shaken his head over, calling Daddy to fix some new scrape she'd gotten herself into.

There was no hope for it—she had to do it. But first, she had to get out of these ridiculous clothes. She riffled through the bag that Rosa had sent and found a pair of black leggings on the bottom. They would certainly be an improvement to the chartreuse capris she'd been wearing all day. But there was no other blouse or shirt, so she went to David's drawer and began looking through his meager selection. She chose a dark blue cotton sweater with short sleeves and an open weave. It was huge, the shoulders drooping and the hemline hanging down below her hips, but it looked better than the parrot shirt.

It was time to go down and join David. She hesitated, looking at herself in the mirror. It was strange how much she liked him. Maybe it was because he was completely different from Armand. There was nothing sneaky about David, nothing calculating. There was a core of decency to him that couldn't be denied, despite the dangerous glint he sometimes had in his dark eyes.

She gave a little shiver of appreciation, thinking of that glint. The business with Armand had been a painful blow to her ego, but one smoldering look from David had been enough to build it right back up again. There was no denying the attraction that sparked between the two of them, even though David seemed hell-bent on blotting it out.

She slipped through the room where her children slept and went down the stairs. David was putting away the glassware, wiping off water spots with a white cotton cloth before he set the glasses in neat rows.

She sat down on a stool at the counter and smiled at him. "You asked me why I married Armand," she said simply. "I put you off because it's sort of a painful subject. But I decided I ought to get it out into the open. You've been a good friend to me. If you really want to know, I'll tell you."

David turned to look at her. He supposed it was really none of his business, but he didn't care. He wanted to know.

Throwing down the cloth, he leaned on the counter across from her. "Okay," he said softly. "Shoot."

She folded her hands in front of her and stared at them as she began. "My parents had two children, me and Reed. You know Reed. You know what a great guy he is. My parents have always been so proud of him. There was that one little lapse, when he insisted on going into the army, that nearly broke my father's heart." She threw him a quick grin. "But other than that, he's been their hero, forever and ever."

David nodded. That was certainly the picture he got when he visited the family.

"Well, Reed was perfect. I was the defective one. I'd call it the black sheep, only I never did anything that put me behind bars or anything like that." She cast him a quick smile that had just enough heartbreak in it to give his heart a wrench. "But I was considered scatterbrained. Goofy. Not very bright. The girl most likely to fall in the pool at a party or sit on the cake at a picnic.''

She made a face and David had to struggle to keep from grinning. Something told him she hadn't pulled those examples out of thin air.

"You get the picture, right?"

He nodded.

"I sort of played up the image while I was still in high school. I mean, it got me out of a lot of pressure. They didn't expect much from me, and I didn't do much that amounted to anything." She sighed, shaking her head as she thought back. "A lot of wasted time, I know. But I was so..." She gave a self-deprecating laugh. "Whoops, I guess I shouldn't fall into that trap myself, should I? The point is, once I turned twenty, I was sick of being the feebleminded member of the family. I tried every way I could to prove to them that I wasn't really like that. But it seemed that their minds were made up. I was a ditzy blonde, and that was all there was to that song.''

She looked at him and shrugged. "And then I met Armand. If you saw him now, it would be hard to explain what it was about him that appealed to me at the time. He was an older man, successful, respected. He fell in love with me right away. And everything changed. All of a sudden I was different in everyone's eyes. I had stature."

David frowned. He didn't get it. "Because of that sleazeball?" he growled.

She shook her head. "Oh, no, you're getting a very false impression of what Armand is like. He's very handsome, very charming. And very presentable."

"Presentable—what the hell does that mean?" And yet he knew, didn't he? Presentable was everything that he himself wasn't.

"It means he's all right," Shelley said. "Don't you understand? He's socially correct. He has money and culture behind him. His mother went to school in Switzerland with my mother. When I was with him, people looked at me with an admiration I'd never seen before. It was wonderful, heady, like drinking champagne."

"But it was based on his reputation, not on anything you'd done."

She laughed at him. "What do we have here, a closet feminist?"

He shrugged, his smile tight. "What can I say? I'm a man of the nineties."

"Well, you're right, of course. But I didn't see it at the time. He was utterly devoted, showering me with attention. Our wedding was gorgeous. The honeymoon was . . ."

She hesitated and he studied her face, trying to read the signs.

"Some slight hints of what was to come surfaced during the honeymoon," she said softly, staring at her hands again. "But I told myself things would smooth over. We needed time to adjust to each other."

She looked up, her eyes wide. "I was in love with him. I can't pretend I wasn't. And I wanted it to work. We had an apartment in Manhattan and a house in Greece. We spent a lot of time on his yacht, sailing to the Greek islands." She smiled. "That part was lovely. We usually had friends along. It was an enchanted time." She paused, closing her eyes for a moment. "Then I had Jill, and everything changed."

"He didn't want children?"

She shook her head. "It wasn't that, really. At least, he said he wanted them. But while I was pregnant he began to . . . stray, shall we say? And once he developed the habit, he didn't seem to be able to break it."

"I see." He hated Armand more all the time.

"I began to have to face that the marriage was falling apart. I got pregnant with Chris by mistake, and that made me determined to try to salvage something. But we drifted farther and farther apart, and finally I left."

"Before Chris was born?"

She nodded. "He didn't contest the divorce. At the time he seemed glad to be rid of me." She held her arms as though she were cold, and the sweater slipped down off her shoulder. She pushed it back right away, but David had caught sight of something dark and ugly.

"Hey," he said, frowning. He rose and came around the counter to where she sat. "What was that?"

She pulled the sweater tight up to her neck with two hands. "Nothing," she said quickly, but her eyes had that haunted look again.

"The hell it was." He forced her hands away and pulled the neck until her shoulder and upper arm were exposed. Large, angry bruises appeared in two areas, bruises that conformed very closely to those that would be made by the fingers of a man's hand.

David stared at the bruises for a moment, white rage almost blinding him. "Did he do this to you?" he asked, his voice like metal against rock.

"David—"

"Did he?"

She closed her eyes and nodded.

His hand tightened on the sweater. "I'll kill the bastard," he said with low menace.

"David—" She pulled the sweater back again. "It's not really as bad as it looks." She gazed up at his face, hard as stone, full of anger, and she put a hand on his arm. "It's not really your problem, you know," she said softly. "Forget it."

He turned his face away, inarticulate with fury. He wanted to damage Armand badly. How any man could touch a woman like this, hurt her... The very idea violated something deep inside him.

"David." Her hand was still on his arm. He looked down, his eyes wary. She smiled, feeling very warm toward him. He was a special guy. "Are you seeing anyone seriously right now?" she asked softly.

He stared at her, thrown off course by her question. "What?"

"Do you have a girlfriend?"

He frowned, unable to see what *that* had to do with. "No. No one serious."

Her smile became more mischievous at the edges, her silver-blue eyes sparkling. "Then why won't you kiss me?" she asked softly.

He stared down at her, his vision blurred. All he saw was her golden hair, her red lips. Reaching out, he touched her cheek with the palm of his hand, as though he were touching a treasure he was afraid he might break.

She was so honest, how could he do anything else but tell her the truth?

"Because if we start something," he said, his voice low and husky, aching with his need for her, "I'm going to have to finish it."

She reached up and put her hand over his, holding him to her. Her other hand lifted and flattened against his chest. "I could risk that," she whispered.

"Shelley..." He pulled her toward him, his pulse beating in his ears. "I'm not one of your upper-crust country-club lovers. I'm too rough around the edges for you, and you know it."

"I think I can handle it, David," she murmured, her lips only inches from his. "Try me."

He'd resisted a lot in the last few hours, but there was no way he could resist this. He'd been breathing in her seductive beauty like the air around him. He'd been reveling in it, tasting it, feeling it. But that had been a dream, and this was reality. And once again, she exceeded expectations.

As his mouth covered hers, she leaned toward him, stretching up to accept him. She was soft and smooth as butter, warm as a hot bath on a frosty day, and he plunged deeper and deeper, as though he were searching for something elusive that he might never find.

He wanted to be rough with her, just a little coarse, show her that he wasn't genteel. But that was impossible. She was such a lady, he had to treat her like one. There was just no other way.

That didn't mean she was demure. There was nothing shy or reserved about the way she kissed him back, the way she pressed her breasts against him, the way her hands slid across his chest. Her touch, her scent, the taste of her, all combined to send his senses reeling.

She murmured something, but he couldn't hear her. There was a roaring in his ears. He could drown in her, set himself adrift and never come back. His hands moved on her, exploring for shape and heat rather than specifics. She was so smooth, so soft . . .

He was probing deeper, her body was so close to his, her hands seeming to pull him tighter, and he was reeling, floating, losing touch with planet Earth.

"David."

Suddenly he realized she'd spoken. She was struggling to free herself, and he pulled back, looking at her groggily, drunk from her seductive charms.

"David, the kids. Don't you hear them?"

No. His senses weren't set on the kid frequency like hers were. But now that she mentioned it, he could hear Chris calling for his mother.

He frowned, trying to catch his breath. He'd been in another world. He hadn't been able to know, see, feel, touch anything but her. He'd been on the edge, about to lose control. Even now he had to force himself to release her.

"David, I have to go to them."

She disentangled herself from his arms, slipped off the stool and hurried up the stairs.

He leaned back against the counter and stared into the void he'd almost fallen into. He felt disoriented, out of touch with reality. What was he, just one giant male hormone? He had to get hold of himself.

He swallowed hard, hating himself. He'd almost done the very thing he feared the most. He'd just about made a complete fool of himself.

What was the matter with him, anyway? How could he be so stupid? He never did things like this. He never lost control. Shelley had him tied up in knots, and he didn't know how to loosen the bonds.

Six

His body was ramrod hard and he had to force himself to breathe evenly to relax. A cold shower seemed like a valuable option. And maybe hara-kiri as well, while he was at it. Why not? He had no self-respect left. Wouldn't that be the honorable way out?

He groaned, closing his eyes. He'd never wanted a woman the way he wanted Shelley. And he wasn't sure he could hold out much longer, telling himself it was the only sane and safe course to follow. After all, he was only human.

"Make that *subhuman*," he muttered, going into the kitchen and getting a tall glass of cold water. Instead of drinking it, he threw it on his face.

Someone was clopping down the stairs and he turned, wiping off the water with a towel. It was only Jill. She grinned and waved at him.

"Hi," she sang out. "Mama's calling Grandpa. Can we come down and stay with you?"

Kids. Their arrival extinguished the flame as well as any shower could. He drew in a ragged breath and managed to grin at the happy little darling.

"Sure. Listen, you and Chris can help me make lemonade. Want to?"

"From real lemons?" Her head cocked to the side with interest.

"The real thing."

She nodded. "What do I do first?"

Chris joined them and David had the two of them using the juicer on the fresh lemons Rosa had brought that morning. Before long, Shelley came down to join them. David couldn't look her in the eye, so he made a lot of jokes and had the children rolling with laughter.

Finally the juice was made with almost as much liquid getting into the pitcher as ended up all over the floor and the two kids. They each had a drink and Shelley sent them upstairs to clean themselves up.

"Messy little game," she noted, watching them go. "You've got a lot to learn about doing things with children." But she smiled at him.

He shrugged, picking up a cloth and wiping down the counters. "I figure it's worth it if they learned something."

She nodded. "You know, you're probably right." She grabbed a cloth and joined him.

He moved farther down the counter so she wouldn't touch him. A man could take only so much.

"So, is your father riding to the rescue?" he asked. A pain like a knife thrust slashed through his chest at the thought of her leaving and yet at the same time, he knew very well it was for the best.

She turned and looked at him, shaking her head, her eyes clouded. "Nope. I was just trying to think of a way to tell you. It looks like we're going to have to beg room and board from you for a few more days. My parents, it seems, have gone to Paris for a week of fashion shopping. Reed is out of town on business. And my father's lawyer is on a fishing trip and won't be back until Monday. As this is Thursday..."

"You'll be here for another three days."

She nodded. "I'm sorry, David. I really am. But I don't know what else we can do."

He wouldn't look at her. He kept on wiping down the counter, his face turned away, and she had no idea what he was thinking.

"David, if this is going to be an inconvenience, maybe you know someone else we could stay with."

He turned toward her, his face unreadable. "I can give you the money," he said shortly. "I didn't bring a lot down here with me, but I'm sure I can scrape together enough for airfare."

"Oh, no." She shook her head emphatically, her hair flying around her face. "No, I will not take your grandparents' money."

He stared at her. "You could always pay it back later," he said quietly.

"No. Definitely not." She looked at him uncertainly. If she were honest, she would have to say she wasn't as disappointed in having to stay as she might have been a few hours ago. The more she got to know David, the more she liked him and the more she enjoyed being with him. Something special seemed to be flowering between them, something exciting, and she didn't want to see it snuffed out before it had a chance to grow.

What she didn't like was staying so close to Armand's influence. That frightened her. But he'd already had his flunky come by and didn't find her—and David made her feel safe. And the kiss they'd shared had given promise of an intimacy that might develop if she gave it half a chance.

Usually that would make her run in the opposite direction. But there was something in David's kiss that made her want to stay and explore the possibilities. The trouble was she was getting very bad vibes at the moment. Anyone watching David might almost think he could hardly wait to get rid of her.

He didn't do anything to dispel that feeling. Turning away, he went back to cleaning without another word on the subject.

And the truth was he didn't know what to say. His emotions were in such a tangle he wasn't sure what he wanted.

Her. He wanted her. That much was obvious. His body was tortured with yearning, and his soul had developed a hunger he wasn't sure any woman could satisfy.

But why was it so different with Shelley? He'd been crazy about other women. He'd had crushes, had infatuations. He'd lusted and loved, in a fashion. This was so different. It cut deeper, seemed more intense, more dangerous.

Maybe it really wasn't her. Maybe it was what she represented—the wealth and ancestors, the mansions and debutante teas, the European schools and important connections. After all, didn't she stand for everything that he could only admire from afar, everything that he could never reach and hold in his hand because of who he was, the way he'd been brought up, where he came from? Shelley was exotic. She was fantasy. And he was afraid to fall in love with her.

Of course, he wasn't *really* in love. He was *obsessed,* that was all. Obsessed and demented. He would never fall in love with the woman. That would be even more insane. He had to draw the line somewhere.

Falling in love with her would be like falling in love with an angel. You couldn't touch an angel. You couldn't hold her. You couldn't make love to her. You could only dream and stare at an angel from the ground. You couldn't fly, just because you loved her.

And that was what he would be doing if he continued with this stupid obsession.

The kids came down and began to help David make dinner, Jill sweeping the floor, Chris folding napkins and Shelley learning to cook. Her mishaps brought on laughter, and before he knew it, David was joking with her again, as though they were old friends instead of uneasy almost-lovers.

He taught Shelley how to make red rice and then a cream chili sauce that would go with his fish steaks that evening. She stirred the sauce until it looked like liquid silk and then she showed it off.

"I'm getting so good at this cooking stuff, I just may have to try doing some of it when I get home," she said as everyone praised it. "Next, baked Alaska."

"How about enchiladas rancheras for a warmup?" David suggested. "I need a pan of them." He gestured toward the counter. "There are the tortillas. And there's the cooked chicken."

She only hesitated a moment before tackling the job. Jill helped for a while, then retreated to a table with her notebook. Chris played with little boxes he was pretending were cars on the dining room floor, while David made the sauce and kept a watchful eye on Shelley.

"This is really fun," she announced when she produced a pan of fairly decent-looking enchiladas. "I just may have a knack for being a happy homemaker after all."

"Maybe you should get married again," David said without thinking, and then regretted it immediately.

She looked at him. "Oh?" She raised an eyebrow, but otherwise didn't seem to take offense. "What makes you say a thing like that?"

He looked at her steadily. "Well, I hear there are plenty of men chasing after you in San Diego."

Her mouth dropped open and her eyes widened. "Where did you hear a thing like that?"

The tiniest twinkle appeared in his dark eyes. He shrugged casually. "Jill and I were discussing it."

She sank onto a stool at the counter. She liked it when he wasn't trying to be off-putting. "Oh you were, were you?" She threw her daughter a look of mock ferocity that made Jill giggle.

"Yeah, we were." He gave Jill a wink, wiping his hands on a dish towel. "From what I heard, it sounded like this Kyle Tanner guy—the race car driver—has the inside track." He looked at her, watching her eyes, wondering how she was going to react. "Unless there's somebody else Jill doesn't know about."

Shelley sputtered, looking from David to her daughter and back again, at a loss for words. "What?" she managed to utter at last. But she was enjoying the teasing. Anything to keep David smiling.

He went on blithely. "Of course, we mustn't forget Cubby, the kids' favorite," he noted, still watching her, hoping for clues. She really wasn't giving anything away.

"Cubby!" Shelley shook her head, trying not to laugh.

Chris sat up, clapped his hands together and started a chant. "We want Cubby. We want Cubby."

Jill joined in with less enthusiasm, just to make people laugh.

Shelley turned and gave David a significant look. "They want Cubby," she noted wryly.

He nodded. "Yes, I got that impression before." He moved closer, looking down at her. "The question is—do you want Cubby?"

She looked at him challengingly, her eyes a silver screen. "The answer is—none of your business."

He grinned, brushing her hair back off her cheek with a negligent touch that came so naturally, he didn't let himself think twice about it. "Well, that Jim fellow sounded like sort of a jerk. I think you should forget about him."

She liked his touch. She liked the way he'd brushed aside her hair, as though they'd moved to a new state of familiarity. But she wasn't so sure about the advice.

Her eyes flashed. "Jim is a very decent man. He does very well financially, and he has a great sense of humor."

David laughed. "A great sense of humor. Wow, snap him up."

She pretended defiance. "Maybe I will," she said.

Jill and Chris both groaned.

"See, they don't want him," David commented with a grin. "He thinks he can buy you with presents."

She stared back at him. "How do you know I'm not for sale?" she said softly.

He stared back at her. "Some things are just too precious to barter with," he said back, so softly only she could hear him.

Their gazes clung and she was short of breath. When she finally pulled away, it was his mouth she couldn't stop looking at.

"Anyway," Jill was saying in the background, "I don't like him."

She blinked, trying to remember who Jill was talking about, then turned and looked at her daughter, steadying herself. "Why don't you like Jim?"

Jill shrugged and squinted at her mother. "Because he always wants us to go stay overnight somewhere else so he could be alone with you," she told her.

"Oh." Shelley blanched and sighed. "You told David about that?"

Jill nodded. "I showed him my notebook."

Shelley shuddered. "That damn notebook," she muttered, giving David a look.

"You know about her lists?" he asked, laughter shining in his eyes.

Shelley nodded. "She's a very organized girl. I just wish she wouldn't try to organize *my* life."

He leaned on the counter, close enough to smell the scent of her hair. He was enjoying this. He could get close and almost touch her, and yet know he wasn't in danger of doing anything he was going to regret. He couldn't go any further, with the children in the room.

"I guess you were never the type to make lists in notebooks," he said to her.

She laughed, half-turning to look into his face. "No, not me. I've always been more the 'let's just ride this wave and see what happens' type." She smiled into his eyes, and for a moment he had the uneasy feeling she was trying to tell him something. "I never kept a notebook in my life."

David crossed his arms over his chest and smiled, but his head went back as though he were trying to distance himself a little from whatever she might mean. "Well, that is some interesting notebook Jill keeps," he went on. "It makes it pretty clear old Tanner's at the head of the pack." His eyes sharpened as he watched for her reaction. "After all, you went to France with him."

She turned slowly until she was facing him directly and stared at him. "I went to France with him?" She blinked and laughed aloud. "Yes, I guess I did do that. My, how risqué of me."

Damn. He'd hoped she would deny it. Or give some platonic explanation. Despite everything he suddenly felt grumpy again. "So I guess he's it, huh? Unless . . . unless there's somebody else."

She held his gaze with her silver-blue eyes. "There just might be."

He swallowed hard, not sure he wanted to go on with this. "Who?"

The tiniest of smiles curled the very edges of her mouth. "I'm not going to tell you."

She was teasing him. Her eyes were flirting. Did she really want him to think that he was the one she was talking about? No, he must have it wrong. She was just having a little fun at his expense. But then, why was she still holding his gaze, her eyes like crystal caverns, deep and limitless, mysterious and enticing? He wanted to reach out and hold her, take her in his arms, stroke her hair.

"I'm making a new page," Jill announced, breaking the spell between them.

They both sat up a little straighter and blinked, then looked toward the girl.

"Who . . . who is it for?" Shelley asked shakily.

"David," Jill said matter-of-factly.

They both turned fully and stared at her.

"David?" Shelley repeated, her voice slightly hoarse.

Jill nodded like an efficient researcher in mid-search. "I already wrote that he is very handsome. What else shall I put?"

Shelley and David looked at each other, and the teasing light was back in her eyes. "I know something," she said, her voice full of laughter. "Why don't you put down this . . ." She paused, playing on the suspense of the moment. "Here it is—he's a real good kisser."

"Mama!" Jill blurted out in shock.

"Shelley!" David did the same.

But Jill recovered quickly. "Mama, how do you know?"

Shelley looked wide-eyed and innocent as she answered her daughter. "He told me so himself." Then she grinned. "And I believe him."

He was blushing again. Wasn't this the third time in the last twenty-four hours? And probably the third time in his life. Being with Shelley had activated flushing capabilities he hadn't known he had. "I never said that," he claimed weakly.

Jill giggled, ducked her head, and began to write it down.

Laughing softly, Shelley watched with delight as he reddened again. Then he reached out quietly and grabbed her hand, lacing his fingers with hers, and leaned close to her ear, drawing in her scent, losing himself in the silver mist of her hair.

"Just wait until later," he whispered. "You're going to have to pay for that little jab."

"Why?" she whispered back, her breath soft and warm on his cheek. "You going to try to prove me wrong?"

He opened his mouth, but there was really nothing he could say to that, and they both laughed, holding hands tightly. He drew back a little, but he couldn't stop gazing into her eyes, as if the rest of the world would fade away if he just stared long enough. She looked back, her eyes full of laughter, but with something else lurking at the edges, something more serious that seemed to be asking a question.

What was the question? He wasn't sure, and it nagged at him for the rest of the afternoon. He went out to get supplies and saw some friends, but he hardly gave them more than a nod and a wave. He had other things on his mind.

Shelley, to be specific. She was on his mind and in his soul and definitely the main concern of his raging libido. He was getting too friendly with her. That was dangerous. He had to cut it out.

"Tell you what," he told her when he got back, as he unloaded the groceries. "I don't think you should get married at all."

She looked up from the soup she was stirring, surprised. "No? Why not?"

He stopped by and looked down at the soup. "Because marriage is just a trap. Didn't you find that out for yourself? It's just a modern form of legalized slavery." He looked into her eyes. "It should be abolished. Done away with."

She gazed at him levelly. "I see. You're a confirmed bachelor. Is that right?"

"Of course. Marriage is for morons."

"And you're too smart, too strong, to opt for a life like that."

"Now you're getting it."

She licked her lips. "Does that also mean you don't think you need a woman in your life?" she challenged.

But before he could follow up on that one, another voice was heard from.

"You know what, Mama?" Jill piped up from the counter where she was shelling peas. "David has lots of girlfriends."

Shelley and David turned to look at her.

"What?" Shelley asked,

Jill nodded seriously, her sharp-eyed gaze going from one of them to the other. "Rosa told me about them when she was putting us to bed."

David was beginning to feel violated. He frowned with apprehension. "What did she tell you?"

Jill threw him a fleeting smile, but she was really talking to her mother. "She told me about all the girls that come around to flirt with David."

David moved impatiently. "Rosa's got to learn discretion," he muttered.

But Shelley was laughing again, teasing David with a wide-eyed glance. "Go on, Jill. What did Rosa tell you about these girls?"

David turned, alarmed. "Hey, maybe she'd better not..."

"Oh?" Shelley's eyebrows were both sky high this time. "Been a little 'risqué' yourself, have you?"

He looked at her helplessly, shaking his head.

She grinned, but took pity on him. "Don't worry. I'm sure Rosa didn't tell X-rated things to the children."

"I'm glad you're sure," he murmured, sinking back against the counter in resignation.

Shelley patted his hand, then left her fingers there to curl around his. "Go on, Jill."

Jill went on. "Rosa said that all the girls in town come in their best dresses and eat here so David can look them over."

Shelley gave him a skeptical look. "*All* the girls in town?" she asked.

"Rosa exaggerates," he muttered gloomily, feeling gallows-bound.

"Then she says David picks the prettiest one and takes her out."

"Sexist pig," Shelley murmured for only him to hear.

"Rosa's wrong," he claimed. His gloom evaporated as he gave her a quick grin. "I always give them IQ tests. Honest. The smartest girl wins, no matter what she looks like."

Shelley made a face at him, and then stopped Jill before she went on.

"Jill." Shelley put up her hand, laughing. "Let's not torture David anymore. Save the rest for later. It's almost time to open for the evening meal. We want him functional for that, at least."

"Okay." Jill hopped down off her chair and began to gather her things. "Come on, Chris. Let's go upstairs. I'll tell you a story."

Chris looked up from playing with his pretend cars, finally interested. " 'Bout the flying trantulas?" he asked.

"Okay. Let's go."

They trudged off. David didn't even bother to ask about the spider stories. He'd heard enough from Chris to know the explanation wouldn't make any sense, anyway.

"I can see I'm going to have to have some conversations with Rosa myself," Shelley was teasing, leaning back and looking at him through narrowed eyes. "She seems to know everything there is to know about you."

He gave her a baleful look. "The trouble with Rosa is, some of the things she knows never really happened. So take anything she says with a grain of salt."

Shelley laughed. Tales of David's old girlfriends didn't really bother her. Everybody had a past. "She's sort of like an aunt to you, isn't she? Have you known her for a long time?"

"Forever. I used to spend my summers down here when I was a kid. She was always here. And I called her 'Tia'."

"All your summers?" She leaned forward, her chin in her hand. "Really?"

He nodded, his eyes growing more distant. It was evident this was not his favorite topic of conversation, but she wanted to know more about him, so she pushed.

"Were your parents traveling or something?" she asked.

He grunted. She would think something like that—she with the family who took off for Paris just to go shopping. "No. My parents were divorced."

Her face changed. "Oh, David, I'm sorry."

He shrugged. "Don't be. I survived."

But had he really? She could see the wariness in his eyes. Children of divorce were always damaged to some extent. Usually they got over it pretty well by adulthood. But there were always some residual pangs.

"David." She put a hand on his arm, her eyes dark and compassionate. "Tell me about your parents."

He looked around for an excuse not to. But it was still ten minutes until opening, and Rosa hadn't arrived. The children had left the room. He was going to be trapped into talking about something he never talked about—with anyone. He wasn't even sure if he could do it.

Hell, it was none of her business, anyway. What did she care about his parents, or about any of his background? All she was going to learn were more reasons why the two of them didn't belong together. He wouldn't do it. He didn't want to tell her anything.

But when he looked into her eyes, something opened up inside him, and to his surprise he found the words pouring out, as though they had been pent up for much too long.

"My father was Mexican," he told her. "My mother was a school teacher from Kansas. She taught English as a Second Language classes in night school. That was where they met."

"He was her student?"

He nodded. "He was trying to improve his English because he was running his own business, a nursery, and he felt he needed more precision in his speech. And she helped him get it."

Funny, he hadn't thought about that in years. The two of them meeting that way—it was nice. Too bad the good stuff was so short lived. "Anyway, they fell in love. They got married. They had me. They got a divorce."

She was listening closely, trying to feel what he must have felt. "How old were you at the time?"

"Of the divorce? About ten." He hesitated, but she seemed to expect more, and to his surprise, he began to give it to her.

"Just like for most children of divorce, my universe fell apart. It was like I was schizophrenic, like I lived in two different worlds. My mother moved back to Kansas, to her mother's, and part of the year I lived there, with her, living behind a white picket fence, church on Sundays, big dinners with a ton of cousins, dancing lessons, picnics in the park. And then the rest of the year I was in East Los Angeles, watching my father work eighteen-hour days to support us and dodging homeboys who wanted to bash in my head because I wouldn't join their gang."

A smile twisted his wide mouth, remembering. "When I was in Kansas I felt guilty for leaving my father all alone in the barrio. And when I was back there, I felt like a traitor to my mother. The only times that were really sweet were when I came down here to visit my grandparents. I didn't have to feel guilty about anything then. I just enjoyed life."

"So that's why you love it here. That's why you come back every year."

He shrugged. "That's a big part of it."

The bell on the front door rang. David swung around, relieved. Their talk would have to be declared over. "Okay, now you get to meet Rosa," he said. "Like I said, ignore most of what she has to say about me."

"Not a chance, David." She slid down off the stool, but turned back once more before going forward to meet Rosa. "We can't talk any longer now," she said softly. "But we do have some things we need to discuss. I'll wait up for you."

Wait up for you. The words were like a warning, booming in his head. Something told him she was going to be temptation itself tonight. He was going to have to be careful.

Seven

It wasn't so bad when Shelley was talking to David or reading stories to the kids, but now that she was all alone, sitting in the semidarkness, the bogeyman seemed to be very close to her door.

The last snatches of desultory conversation wafted up from the room below. There were only a few customers left in the café. But she was paying no attention, anyway. Her mind was on Armand right now.

Armand. Who would have believed he would become so menacing in her life? He'd been very sweet when they'd first arrived aboard the yacht, cooing over the children, laughing with her, telling her she looked more beautiful than ever. He'd been his old charming self, the Armand she had fallen in love with all those years ago, the Armand she had married. After the first day, she had actually begun to contemplate what life might be like if they got back together again.

But that hadn't lasted long. After a few days he began to get edgier. One night, after they'd put the children to bed, he brought out a bottle of wine and a couple of candlesticks, and they'd talked of old times. And then he'd kissed her.

There had been something in that kiss that had been repugnant to her, had stirred memories she'd been trying to ignore. When she tried to pull away, his fingers had hardened on her and his temper had flared. He'd never hit her before, even during their worst times in the past, but he did then. He slapped her and shoved her down on the couch and tried to kiss her again, telling her they were going to make love.

Make love. What words to use. As though they weren't divorced. As though there were still some feeling between them. As though the last few years had just melted away.

She told him no, that she didn't feel that way about him anymore. She put her hand over her mouth now, thinking about it. She'd been so scared. She couldn't scream. Everyone else on the yacht worked for him. Besides, she didn't want to wake her children up. She didn't want them to see what he was doing to her. So she struggled in silence, clawing and kicking and squirming away from him in any way she could, and finally he gave up, swearing at her viciously, storming out of the cabin, leaving her alone.

He didn't try to touch her again, but from then on, there was a new look in his eyes. He didn't love her. He hated her. So why, why did he want her back?

He tried to make it up to her the next day with presents. But now she knew what was hiding behind the mask. She'd stayed another day, just to let the children be with him. But then he began to be short with them. He didn't like them any more than he liked her. It was one thing to let them know a parent who cherished them, it was quite another to confuse them by forcing them to be with a father who obviously didn't love them. What would that do to their emotional health?

She decided she had to leave, and that decision hardened when she took a walk around the deck of the yacht and ran across Armand's teenaged girlfriend sunbathing in her bikini. She'd marched back to the cabin and told Armand what she thought of him, then announced she was leaving. He'd laughed, but she hadn't taken in the full implications of his reaction until she asked him for her purse and papers, and he'd laughed again.

"You aren't going anywhere," he'd told her. "I've got you now, Shelley. I told you I wanted you back, and that's the way it's going to be. We're going to be remarried, you and I. Don't look so shocked, darling. Think of it as fate. Your destiny."

But why, why? He didn't love her. She knew he had wanted the divorce just as much as she had. Why this sudden obsession with family togetherness? It didn't make any sense.

And it was terrifying. He seemed to have so many people working for him. He'd always liked a lot of servants around, but this was a new crew. These people had hard, cold faces. They looked as though they'd as soon slit your throat as give you breakfast. She shuddered, thinking of what would have happened if one of them had found her and the children.

Yes, she really needed to get home as quickly as possible. She'd plunged into a nightmare when she'd come down here, and she was still scratching her way back to the surface. Only two things were keeping her here—lack of money... and David.

David. She stretched back and smiled. He was a whole other story. She had to laugh when she remembered how he'd looked at her when she'd first stepped into his apartment. He'd liked what he'd seen. It had shone in his eyes in a way a woman couldn't help but appreciate. And then the protective wall had come down like a steel door. And she'd found that she wanted more than anything to find out why, to make that wall go away.

She'd known a lot of men over the last few years. She'd dated and discarded one after another. There was always something wrong—too attentive, not attentive enough, too arrogant, too timid. She'd begun to think Armand had ruined her, that she would never trust again. But with David...

Maybe he had some flaws, too. Heck, everybody did. She just hadn't known him long enough to see his drawbacks. But she very well knew there was something honest and solid about him. When he said things to her, even if he were angling for something, she knew he was speaking from the heart. Who could resist a man like that?

She sighed and curled up in the corner of his couch, waiting for him to come up. They had a few things to talk over. Maybe he could help her puzzle out this problem with Armand. Maybe not. But she wanted to talk to him. Her eyes drifted closed, and she waited.

It was an hour after closing before David finally turned off the lights. He'd done just about everything he could think of to avoid going upstairs. There was nothing left to do. But there hadn't been a sound from upstairs in a long, long time. And Shelley would have come down by now if she were still awake. So maybe it was actually safe to go up. He certainly hoped so.

He climbed the stairs quietly, and turned on the landing. And there she was, sound asleep, curled up in his shirt again, right in the middle of his couch. He stared down at her, his heart thumping. She looked small and vulnerable and unbelievably tantalizing, like a black and white photograph here in the shadows, like a piece of art. He wanted to pick her up and hold her in his arms. If only there was some way to do that without waking her up.

Leaning down over her, he put a hand on her shoulder and shook gently. "Shelley," he said. "Wake up."

She stirred and stretched, and his shirt fell open, revealing one perfectly formed breast. He drew in air as though he'd just been slugged in the stomach and for a second, he didn't think he would be able to breathe. She was the most beautiful sight he'd ever seen.

There was no way to stop his hand; he was beyond that kind of control at the moment. He touched her, the backs of his fingers sliding from the top of her breast to the rose-colored tip, all shiny and soft and relaxed. Her eyelids fluttered, and he cupped her breast in the palm of his hand, every part of him aching for her.

"David?"

She smiled up at him, her eyes sleepy. Instead of pulling away, she reached for him, her hands meeting behind his neck and tugging him down. At the same time, she straightened on the couch and the crisp shirt rode up, exposing her leg all the way to the hip.

She wasn't surprised. David's hot looks and her spontaneous response had seemed natural right from the beginning, in a way it had never seemed with any other man.

It wasn't just that he wanted her. She was an attractive woman, and she ran across that generic sort of desire all the time. It was more that she wanted him back. That didn't happen very often. In fact, except for Armand, when she'd first known him, it didn't happen at all. And she was older now, better able to judge character and value, and she knew David had both. In spades.

She wanted David. And all her life she had pretty much ended up with whatever she wanted. That was just the way life was for a Brittman.

She accepted David with a lazy sense of pleasure, moving to give him room on the couch, hooking a leg over his hip when he lay down facing her, dropping kisses on his rough cheek, until she found his mouth and opened to him.

He was hot and sweet and she couldn't get enough of his taste, his hands on her skin, his clean, masculine scent. He began to unbutton the shirt and she helped him, nipping at his lips with her own, moving against his long, hard body, feeling his growing excitement beneath her hand, urging it on with her touch.

He groaned, quivering, and she laughed softly, loving the feeling of power she had over him, knowing it wouldn't last, but enjoying it while it did. She had him in the palm of her hand. That made her breath come very fast.

He went still for a moment. "The kids..." he murmured near her ear.

She shook her head. "They're asleep," she whispered back. "They're sound sleepers. They won't wake up. It's okay."

And he sank his hands into her again, holding her with a sensual satisfaction, like a primitive triumph from the hunt. She was his for the moment, his to have and to hold... and to love. It was almost too much to take in—like an overview of heaven.

He was shaking. Why was he shaking? When her hand touched his skin, sliding down across his chest and flattening over his navel, he felt the shivering again, coming from deep inside, and he realized it was a manifestation of his need for her, his anticipation.

And then she whispered something to him about protection.

There was no logical reason why that should stop him cold. But it did.

Protection. She needed protection from him all right, protection from his hunger. And he needed protection from what she could do to his heart and soul.

He closed his eyes, swore harshly and jackknifed away from her.

"What is it?" She sat up and stared at him in the gloom. The pale light seemed to find her breasts, illuminating them. "What's the matter?"

He turned his head away. "Cover up, Shelley," he advised evenly. "You'd better get back to bed. We can talk in the morning."

She pressed the shirt to her chest. "What did I do?" she asked softly.

"Nothing." He turned back and looked at her and wanted to touch her hair, reassure her with an arm around her shoulders, but he didn't dare. There was still too much adrenaline pumping through his veins.

"David..." She snagged his hand with her own and brought it to her cheek. "Why not?"

He opened his mouth and then couldn't say it. Instead, he muttered, "Because... because you're Reed's sister...."

Her eyes widened. "That's ridiculous. We're way beyond that."

"I know." He pulled his hand away from her, though it was almost as difficult to do as his previous denial. "And that's just the trouble."

He turned and went into the bathroom. This time the cold shower was a necessity.

Morning didn't change anything. Rain was pattering on the roof. The humidity made the air feel like marshmallow cream, heavy to breathe. Shelley woke up, looked around the room and whispered, "I'm getting out of this place."

The way David had rejected her the night before still rankled her. Nobody liked rejection. She hated it, personally. And she certainly wasn't used to it.

But aside from general self-pity, she couldn't understand it. She knew he liked her. And she knew he wanted her. The evidence had been more than graphic. And for the first time in years she'd been receptive. When she stopped to think how long it had been since she'd even enjoyed a kiss, much less made love with a man—well, there were blizzards warmer than her love life.

Not that she'd minded, really. She'd made up her mind to dedicate herself to being a mother. After all, her children needed double love—they only had her.

She looked at the two tousled heads on either side of her and smiled. In spite of everything, she would do it all again, including marrying Armand, to get these two rascals. Right now, they were all she lived for.

She dressed before she went downstairs this time, pulling on the sweater and black leggings. There was no point in pretending that there was anything growing between her and David. He was obviously determined to nip their attraction for each other in the bud.

"So much for you, David Coronado," she muttered to herself as she dressed. "If that's the way you feel, you can just go on your merry way without us."

David was hardly merry. In fact, he was in a very black mood. He'd already snarled at two early-morning delivery boys and had almost kicked one of the alley cats as it tried to streak past him into the café. Now he was staring into his coffee and thinking about jumping off the nearest cliff.

He was probably the biggest sap on the face of the earth. A beautiful, desirable woman had opened her arms to him last night, and he'd turned her down. And why? Why?

Damned if he knew. He kept trying to bring the situation into focus, but he couldn't make any sense of it.

Did he like the woman? Yes. Did he want to make love to her? Of course. Did he want to hold her and caress her and make her feel wonderful, too? Absolutely. Did she seem willing to give it a try? No doubt about it.

So what the hell was the holdup?

Well, okay. She was rich, for one—a socialite from a prominent family. She'd been to the best schools. She'd run around with jet-setters. She was, in other words, *totally* out of his league.

So what was he saying here, that it was a class problem? They were both supposed to be Americans. Class wasn't supposed to be something you were born into. Your place in life should be determined by what you'd made of yourself.

And he'd done pretty well, if he had to blow his own horn for a bit. He'd gone to a state university instead of a fancy private college, but he'd graduated with honors and worked hard. He had his own firm now, with employees and contracts that could keep him busy for years.

Didn't all that count? Didn't it?

He threw a glass against the wall, just to see it break. Hell, yes, it counted.

But somewhere in the back of his mind was the picture of his mother, sobbing by the telephone in Kansas, and his father, making his own sandwich at five in the morning before he went off to run his nursery in Los Angeles. Two people, two different backgrounds. It just didn't work.

But wait, he argued with himself again. We're not asking you to marry the girl. Just make love with her. This doesn't have to be anything long-term. Just have some closeness now, while you can.

And that was when he realized the truth. More than anything else, he was terrified. He was so damn scared, it made him shake. The truth was he was deeply afraid that if he ever really had her, he would never be free of her again.

"Coward," he said aloud, looking at the coffee cup and considering smashing it like he had the glass. "Coward," he said again, louder, and suddenly Shelley was there, and he knew that she'd heard him.

He rose and went to the sink, holding his breath. He would not blush again, no matter what.

She hesitated for a moment, then thought better of commenting on his name-calling. "Good morning," she said with calm efficiency. "Mind if I pour myself some coffee?"

He turned and looked at her, his eyes huge and shadowed, as though he hadn't been getting much sleep lately. "Sure. Go right ahead."

"I'll just make a couple of pieces of toast and take them up to the kids for their breakfast."

"Fine. Whatever you want."

He was being so accommodating. How was she going to fight with him if he wouldn't be mean? She turned and watched him while the bread toasted. He was breaking eggs into a bowl one by one, as if every egg were someone he had known whose head needed cracking.

"I hate to ask you any more favors," she said coolly, "but it looks like I'm going to have to. I'm in need of a babysitter. Would you mind watching Jill and Chris again in an hour or so?"

He didn't look up. "Why? Are you going back to the banks?"

"No." She took a deep breath. "I'm going out to the yacht to get my purse and papers back."

"What?" One of the eggs he was holding slipped from his hands and hit the floor with a juicy splat, but he didn't notice. "Are you crazy? You can't go out there."

She lifted her face in a characteristic gesture, nose in the air, silver blond hair streaming around her. "What else am I going to do? I can't stay here."

"Shelley..." He took a step toward her and then stopped himself.

"It's perfectly obvious that you want to get rid of me. I'm in the way, I'm an intrusion in your life." She tossed her hair back. This was better. She'd wanted a fight and it looked like she was going to get one. "I'm not used to being an annoyance to someone. And I don't like it. I'm getting out of here."

"No. No, you're not." He didn't sound angry, just sure of himself. He stood before her, his shoulders wide as the sky, his eyes hard, his face like steel, and he suddenly seemed very, very large. "You're not going anywhere."

She met his gaze with no hesitation, but it took effort. She hadn't realized how much bigger he was, how much stronger, until now. But she couldn't let him know she'd noticed. She had to be firm. "I can do what I want to do, David. You can't stop me."

But he was just as unmovable, his voice hard and unsympathetic, brooking no nonsense. "You're going to do what I tell you to do."

Her eyes opened wide with shock. She'd hardly expected this. "Oh really? And what gives you any authority over me?"

He took a step closer, almost touching her, then reached out and took hold of her upper arm, holding lightly, but making his point. "I'm not waiting for anyone to 'give' it to me, Shelley. I'm taking it."

Outrage almost rendered her speechless. A sarcastic "Oh, big man" was all she could come up with right away. She was breathless, not sure where to go from here. He was so close, so domineering, and she was getting flustered. She had to strike back somehow, to show him she wasn't going to let him control her. She pulled away from his hand on her arm. "I guess manhandling a woman will build up your ego. Good luck."

His eyes glittered dangerously. "At least I don't have to depend on other people for my self-esteem."

That was a slap at her, a reference to things she'd told him in confidence. She went white with fury.

"I'm going." She turned, starting toward the stairs. "You can't watch me every minute. You can't keep me here."

In two quick strides, he caught up with her and took her by the shoulders, turning her to face him. He stared down at her for a moment, emotions hidden, but churning inside him. His fingers tightened.

"You're right, Shelley. I can't keep you here." An idea flashed in his dark eyes. "Short of locking you up, anyway."

She gasped. "You wouldn't dare!"

His eyes narrowed with scorn. "I'd dare, all right. But I wouldn't be able to live with myself." He hesitated, staring into her crystal eyes. "Nope, there's only one solution to this deadlock, Shelley."

She was sure she didn't want to hear this, but what else could she say? "What's that?" she demanded, and managed to put some defiance in her tone.

His head went back and he stared at her. "If you go, I go with you."

"No." Her reaction was instantaneous and wrenching, and she reached out to put a hand on his chest, not thinking. "Oh, David, no, you can't go there. God only knows what he might do to you. You might get hurt."

He sighed and shrugged. "There. That's exactly why I won't let you go either. You might get hurt."

"No, David. Don't you see?" There was genuine fear in her eyes. "Armand won't hurt me. He wants me to marry him again. But you...those men who work for him are...they're just like gangsters."

He shook his head, looking at her, his eyes softening. "And you think I'm going to let you deal with gangsters alone?"

Tears were prickling behind her eyes. She had to fight hard to keep them from showing. "But I can't just wait here for them to find us. Don't you see? I have to challenge this thing, not just sit in a corner and hide."

He touched her hair, his gaze smoky. "What if he grabbed you and held you? What would I do with Jill and Chris?"

"Take them to San Diego immediately."

"Without you?" The back of his hand caressed her cheek. He couldn't help it. When he was close, he had to touch her. "No, Shelley. It wouldn't work."

She closed her eyes, steadying herself to the sensations he conjured up in her at a moment's notice. "This doesn't work, either," she murmured, "and you know it."

"It'll at least keep you safe."

"But for how long?" She shook her head, looking up at him again, her eyes apprehensive. "You don't want me here, David. Not really. Face it. I'm just a bother to you."

He groaned, pulling her toward him. "You know damn well you bother the hell out of me," he told her huskily, "but that doesn't mean I don't want you here."

She melted into his arms and his kiss, releasing her doubts, extinguished her anger. His mouth was warm and urgent, his need still unfulfilled, and she knew in that moment that the time would come when he would let her do something about it.

Bumping noises on the stairs announced the imminent arrival of the children, and they drew apart, but Shelley was breathless, staring up at David with a question in her eyes.

As though he could read what she needed to know, he kissed her again, quickly, and whispered, "Shelley, I don't want you to leave." His arms held her closely, then released her. "Don't leave me," he said softly, his dark eyes velvet-deep with emotion. "Not yet."

Her heart was beating wildly as she left him to go see about her children. There was one thing for certain. David's rejection of her the night before had nothing to do with how he felt about her. It had to be something else, something she didn't understand. And maybe it was about time she let go of the concern for her own feelings and thought about his for a change.

Eight

The day passed slowly. The rain cleared up, and then the sun came out and everything sparkled. Shelley could hear all the voices in the café during lunch, but she had to stay upstairs, wishing she could go down and help, but not daring to. If anyone saw her and reported to Armand...

She and the children read stories and played games until they were all sick of each other. And all the time she was thinking, her mind jumping from one thing to another.

Armand was still searching for them, she was sure of it. And he would find them eventually. It was inevitable. Someone would talk, someone in the neighborhood who'd seen them through the big front windows. They hadn't been careful enough at first.

She began to picture various scenarios, of what might happen, but the one that stuck with her was the one where Armand and his henchmen burst through the front door and David sprang up to defend her. They wouldn't hesitate a second in gunning him down. That she was sure of. Then all they would have to do would be to bundle her and the kids on the yacht and head for international waters. Simple as that.

She turned icy cold thinking of it. No, she couldn't let that happen.

She was just coming out of the shower when she heard David arriving upstairs, so lunch had to be over. She heard him tell Jill and Chris they could go down now, and they cheered and ran for the stairs. Then his knock came on the bathroom door.

"Shelley? You in there? I've got something to tell you."

"I'll be right out," she called, whipping a thick towel around herself and tucking it in under her arm. "Just a second."

She opened the door and stood there, her hair twisted in a knot at the top of her head, and nothing on but a turquoise towel that barely skimmed her bottom.

David took one look and turned away, looking pained. "Ah, Jeez, Shelley, do you have to do this to me all the time?"

Her eyes were wide, all innocence. "What do you mean, all the time? This is the very first time I've appeared before you in a towel. The first time ever."

"You know what I mean." He tried to look back, then couldn't look away again. "Shelley..." he said softly, a drowning man.

She had no pity. Her chin came up and her tone was forceful, despite the twinkle in her eyes. "What's the big deal, David? You came out to meet me with nothing on but your robe when I first arrived, and I was able to handle the shock like an adult. Why can't you?"

His eyebrows rose to the challenge. "You handled it, did you?" he retorted, half teasing, his hand reaching out to brush a wisp of hair hovering against her lips. "You think I didn't see the look in your eyes? Face it, woman, you were a goner from the moment you saw me."

She choked with outrage and laughter. "Me? I wasn't the one blushing."

His lip curled ruthlessly. "That's because you have no shame."

She gasped, and he reached out to slide his fingers under the edge of the towel. "Better say 'uncle,'" he threatened. "Or this towel is toast."

He was so close she could feel his breath ruffling her hair. She smiled, leaning even closer. "Dare me," she whispered. "And we'll see who blushes first."

His lips hovered so close she could taste him, and she lifted her face—

"Mama!" The cry came from downstairs. "Chris is making faces out the front window at the people on the street."

Shelley sank back, laughing, and David shook his head, looking down at her with undisguised regret. His fingers grazed her cheek as he pulled away.

"I'll go down and keep an eye on them," he told her. "But first—I called around and talked to some people who know people who know about these things, and I picked up some information about your ex-husband."

She nodded slowly. "Tell me all," she said softly.

"It seems Armand's financial empire is in big trouble. The Greek government impounded his shipping company and he owes *big time,* all over the place. My guess is he thought hitching up with you again would put him in line for a financial bailout from your family."

Her smile had a bittersweet line to it. "So it really isn't me he wants. I was pretty sure that was the case."

He touched her shoulder with an awkward pat. "Which makes him about the biggest fool alive," he said huskily. "Anyway, there's more. He's been doing some pretty shady things, I guess, because apparently there's a warrant out for his arrest in the States."

"So that's why he asked us to meet him in Mexico." She forced a crooked grin. "And here I thought it was because he was so romantic."

A line appeared between David's eyebrows, but he didn't comment. "Anyway, that's the scoop. I'll go down and see what your youngest monster is getting into." He started toward the stairs, then turned back and looked at her. "Are you all right?"

"Oh yes." Her smile was wider this time. "Don't think that this hurts me, David. I knew all along he didn't love me anymore. And the feeling is more than mutual."

He gave a short, brusque nod. "Okay then." And he turned and took the steps three at a time.

She looked after him, watching the way he moved, feeling a sense of affection for his sensitivity to her emotions. He was a sweet guy—as well as a very frustrating one. She hadn't figured him out yet. But she planned to learn all there was to know about him.

It was funny. She was usually so wary of men, so afraid they would take something away from her somehow—her newfound independence, her dignity, her self-respect— something. But she never felt that way with David. He was the only man she'd ever known who seemed to be able to accept her for what she was, without wanting her to play a part for him.

Only maybe she was just fooling herself. Maybe he just didn't care enough to make the effort to change her.

"That could be it," she whispered to herself as she began dressing. But she really didn't believe it.

Still, it was a fact that he was resisting the natural chemistry that stirred between them. Why would he be doing that? Another woman, perhaps? Another commitment of some kind? She couldn't put her finger on exactly what it was, but she knew it haunted him somehow, and she wished she could do something to make it go away.

After dressing, she went down and joined the others. This time she and the kids stayed back in the kitchen, away from the view from the front. She was getting more and more wary of Armand's tentacles.

David taught her how to make tacos and burritos, and she was beginning to think she had a knack for cooking. It was amazing the sense of accomplishment one could get from creating an edible meal. She couldn't understand why she'd avoided it all these years. It was fun.

The kids went upstairs to take a nap and David went down to the docks for fresh halibut, and Shelley was alone in the kitchen, humming to herself as she cut up tomatoes for salsa.

A rustling sound from behind made her whirl. The back door was open and a young woman was entering the café. Shelley's throat went dry, and she began to edge her way toward the stairs. She had no idea who this was.

"Hello," the young woman said, eyeing her without a great deal of warmth. She was very pretty, with flaming red hair and a shapely body, emphasized by the short, tight, gold dress. "Who are you?"

"I, uh, listen, I don't know who you are. Can I do something for you?"

The young woman stared at her for a moment, then shrugged and pouted. "I'm Mia," she said rather resentfully. "Where's David?"

She should have known. One of David's many fans, no doubt. At least she knew David—she'd been afraid Armand might be trying a new tactic. She relaxed. "David's not here right now. May I take a message for him?"

The woman gazed at her with a fair share of hostility. "Who are you? A new waitress or something?"

Yes, this had to be a fan, and she was obviously jealous of anyone who might be threatening her place. "I'm a friend of David's," Shelley answered, hiding her smile.

"A friend, huh?" She admired the catlike fingernails of one hand as though appraising the color. "Well, I can believe that. For a minute I thought maybe you and he were—" she shrugged "—you know...but now that I look at you, I can see that couldn't be." She made a face, just this side of mocking. "David likes women with more fire. You know what I mean? I'm sure you're a little too 'white bread' for him."

Shelley was momentarily speechless. Mia seemed to think this was some game of one-upmanship for David's affections, and that she was obviously winning. Finally Shelley found her voice and asked, making the same mocking face back at the woman, "Are you and David...you know...?"

"Sure." She popped her gum and grinned. "We're an item. I know what he likes."

Well, that really twisted the knife. But she would die before she would let Mia see that it stung. "So you said."

Mia frowned. Evidently she didn't much like Shelley's tone. "Tell me," she asked quickly. "Do you have any tattoos?"

"Tattoos?" Shelley blinked, surprised by the question. "No, uh, no, I don't. Why do you ask?"

"I have two tattoos." She nodded, pleased that she'd beaten Shelley again. "Little tigers. One here...and one here." She pointed toward two very private locations on her body.

Shelley winced and shuddered. "Well, how interesting. It must have been very painful," she added, hoping so with all her heart.

Mia gave her a scornful look. "It was worth it. David likes tattoos. They turn him on." She started for the door. "Tell David to give me a call, huh? Tell him I was lonely last night." And with a toss of her thick red hair, she was gone again.

Shelley was still staring after her. She'd never seen such an amazing display of female competitiveness in her life. Was this what she would have to do to fight for David's affections? Well, heck. She'd always been a fighter. She was ready to try anything.

Rummaging in the little suitcase, she found a bright lipstick and a pair of huge hoop earrings, both of which she put on. Then she searched through drawers for a good felt-tip marker and went to work on her arm. She'd always been good at drawing and in no time she had a kitten on the inside of her left arm. She was just finishing up a flower around her belly button when David came in the same door Mia had departed through.

She rose, fluffing her hair and making kissy motions with her brightly painted lips. "Hello, big boy," she cooed, making her hoop earrings swing. "I've missed you, you gorgeous hunk of male flesh." She swung her hip out and blew him a kiss.

David put down the sack and stared at her, looking like a man on the verge of heading for the nearest exit. "What is this?" he asked suspiciously, looking around as though he expected something to jump out at him from the shadows. "What's the gag?"

"Gag?" She laughed artificially, a little too loud. "No gag here, honey. Just a wild, wild woman." She sashayed up and pinched his cheek. "You had a visitor while you were gone. A woman named Mia. She told me all about what turns you on."

He groaned, then grinned, shaking his head as he looked down at her. "She did, did she?" he commented. "And this was her game plan?"

She frowned. "In a manner of speaking. She says it's always worked for her. But she said I needed a lot of work to really get into it. Unfortunately I'm too 'white bread,' you see. Maybe I can dye my hair red. What do you think?"

"I think you're crazy." His hands snaked around her waist and he laughed softly, looking down at her. "But I like it."

"I knew the tattoos would work," she said smugly, grinning back at him.

His grin died. "Tattoos?" he echoed.

She lifted her arm and flexed so the kitten would move. "See? Are you in love yet?"

"Shelley..." Making a face, he covered the little picture with his hand.

"Wait, wait, you've got to see this one...."

But he grabbed her before she had a chance to reveal her newly decorated belly button. "Shelley, I don't need tattoos to turn me on, and you know it. And I like you just the way you are—clean and slick and blond, smelling like a fresh day on the ocean, looking like springtime."

She gazed up at him, suddenly serious, her blue eyes full of ghosts. "Then why is it you'll make love with Mia and you won't make love with me?" she asked softly.

He stared down at her for a long moment before he answered. "Shelley, I've never touched Mia."

"Then she was lying to me?"

"Well, it's either her or me. What do you think?"

But she didn't have to think anymore. His mouth covered hers and she only had to feel as his warmth poured into her.

It was over much too soon, and he was drawing away, going back to unpack the groceries, chatting about nothing much. But she was glowing. Casual affection from David was worth the wait.

David talked on and on, but his mind wasn't on what he was saying. He was just marking time. He knew he was playing Russian roulette here. He had to quit it. But he couldn't resist. She was so tempting. He couldn't keep his hands off her when she was near, even though she scared him like nothing else in his life ever had. It would be best to get her home and out of his sight.

Evening came and went, and she and the children were ensconced upstairs. Rosa and David were greeting guests downstairs before Shelley realized she had been ignoring the most important aspect of what had happened that afternoon. Jealousy had blinded her to the real problem, and that was the fact that Mia had seen her. She might just be feeling a little jealous herself. And if someone were to show her a picture and ask, Mia would probably send them right over. Shelley drew her breath in sharply when she thought of it. If she'd been smart, she would have stayed upstairs where she belonged.

But she couldn't stay up here forever. She was going stir-crazy as it was. And so were the kids. They couldn't hide this way forever. Puerto Vallarta was a small town. Sooner or later Armand would figure out where they were, whether anyone told him or not. And when he did . . .

The nightmare scenario flashed through her mind again, the one where Armand came crashing in the front door of the café and David lunged forward to protect her, the one where guns blazed and David ended up in a pool of blood on the floor. She closed her eyes to blot that picture away, but it wouldn't go. She was a sitting duck, and David was doomed if she stayed here like this.

No, she couldn't stand it anymore. She couldn't just stay here, waiting to be found by Armand. She had to take the bull by the horns. It was the only way. She glanced across the room at her sleeping children and rose quietly, slipping down the stairs and waiting in the shadows until Rosa came bustling past. Then she gestured to the older woman and set her shoulders. It was time to stop playing the mouse in this cat and mouse game.

It wasn't until sometime later that David began to notice Rosa disappearing for moments at a time at odd intervals. Finally, when he had a moment free, he followed her and found her climbing the stairs.

"Hey," he called up softly. Rosa jumped, put a hand to her heart and came marching back down.

"Don't scare me like that," she scolded. "I could have done cartwheels right back down and knocked you flat. You never know."

"What were you going up there for?"

She hesitated and looked sheepish. "To check on those kids. You know how darling they look when they're sleeping. I don't know, I just had a lull and instead of taking a break out back I decided to..."

Suddenly it was all very clear to David. He gripped her arm, a white line around his mouth. "Where did she go?" he demanded.

She tried to look innocent, but on her it didn't wash. "David, who said—"

"Don't play with me, Rosa. She went somewhere and got you to check on her kids, right?"

Rosa sighed, her shoulder drooping. "She said she'd be back as soon as..."

A pulse was beating in his temple. "Where did she go?"

"I don't know where, David, I swear to you. She said she had to go out and take care of something and she didn't want you to know because you would worry."

He swore viciously, turning away from her, smashing the flat of his hand against the wall. "Damn her, damn her." He turned back quickly. "I'll have to close up. You stay with the kids. Don't leave them for a minute. You understand?"

Rosa looked frightened. "David, what is it? What's going on?"

"Nothing." He tried to calm himself down, at least for outward appearances. There was no point in getting Rosa as upset as he was. "Nothing, really. Just do as I ask. Please."

She nodded, looking worried, and he went back out into the café. There were still four tables with patrons, but everyone was just about finished eating. He hustled them out the door as quickly as he could, ignoring their startled objections, packing up any remaining food in boxes and handing it out, muttering something about an emergency in the family. And then he pulled off the apron and reached for his car keys.

The hook was empty, of course. She'd taken the car. But that wasn't so bad. It would help him pinpoint her location. Not waiting another moment, he was out the door and down the street, jogging at a steady clip, heading for the marina.

He knew where the yacht was. In fact you couldn't miss her. She was one of the largest yachts he'd ever seen, a cruiser, over a hundred feet long. He could only guess at how many people she could accommodate. He'd been at the marina twice in the past two days to check it out. He'd hoped to catch a glimpse of Armand, but he didn't think that he'd done that. There was always someone hanging around the yacht, looking like a thinly disguised guard. But the men he'd seen looked like hoods, and despite everything he thought about Armand, he doubted if he looked quite that much of a lowlife.

It didn't take long to get to the marina. The night was dark, but the lights of the boats were reflected on the inky water like a symphony of fireflies. David spotted his car along the side of the road. Shelley was here all right.

He went by to check it out, hoping against hope that she would be sitting there, thinking things over, but the car was empty. As he turned toward the *Lucky Princess,* dread stuck like a lump in his throat.

Lights were on in some of the cabins. He hesitated in the shadows, trying to see some sign of Shelley, but he didn't see anything, not even a guard. She had to be in there somewhere. Grimacing, he started for the plank set down for access. He was going aboard.

The alarm went off the minute his foot touched the plank, and his first impulse was to turn and run. But he couldn't do that. Shelley was in trouble. She needed him. So he kept going, fully expecting the guard who came catapulting onto the deck from the left, expecting to feel cold steel on his neck and the hard thunk of wood as his spine hit the outer wall of the cabin when the guard slammed him back against it.

"You're trespassing, friend," the grating voice of the guard told him as he held him fast, the gun pressed just under his ear. "I think you took a wrong turn."

"You're a real friendly bunch, aren't you?" David replied, reaching up to push the barrel of the gun away. "Do you welcome all your visitors this way?"

The man backed off just a little, enough to let David straighten up against the wall, but he didn't put away the gun. "What do you want?" he asked coldly, his close-set eyes red in the lantern light. "Who are you?"

"I want to see Armand Alexiakis," David said. There didn't seem much else he could possibly ask for. "My business is with him."

"It's a little late for business, friend. Mr. Alexiakis has already retired for the night."

"Has he?" David's gaze slid away from the hood's eyes and ran across the deck and then focused on the porthole. Shelley had to be here. Where the hell was she? Did Armand have her locked up somewhere? Or was she loose, slithering through the shadows? If only he knew for sure, he would have a better idea of what would work here.

"Why don't you tell him I want to see him? See if he's still awake." And see if he's got Shelley with him. That's all I want to know.

"Why should I?" the hood sneered. "You still haven't told me who you are."

David glanced down the deck again. For just a moment he thought he saw something move. But the harder he stared, the more it looked like simple shadows. He looked away, not wanting to draw attention.

"My name is Jesse Larimer," he said quickly. "I heard your boss was looking for information."

That should bring out something. Either they had Shelley and didn't need an informant any longer, or they didn't and would still want anything that hinted at where she was.

The man's eyes narrowed and he waved the gun. "You got information? Spill it. I'll let you know if we're interested."

Well, that didn't tell him much. He'd have to play coy for a bit longer. "No way." David held out his hand. "Mind if I go into my pocket?"

"What for?" the hood said suspiciously.

"I've got a card to show you."

The red eyes smoldered. "Okay. Take it slow."

David reached in and pulled out the card Armand's man had left at the café the day before.

"See here? Some guy came into my place yesterday and gave me this. Said if I heard anything about a certain party, to get in touch with Mr. Alexiakis." He shrugged. "So here I am."

The hood squinted at the card and seemed to take it at face value. "So tell me already. I'll pass it on to Mr. A."

David shook his head. "I've got nothing to say to anyone else but the boss," he told the man.

The gun was back at his neck, and none too gently. "Then you've got nothing to say, period. You're out of here, mister."

David tried to turn. He couldn't leave, not yet. There was another movement down at the end of the deck and he was careful not to look at it. He definitely didn't want this creep noticing.

The barrel of the gun jabbed into his neck. "Come on. Scram."

And suddenly a new voice cut into the night.

"Cavon, what's going on out here?"

The hood froze, obviously afraid of the man coming out on deck. The stranger was tall, his dark hair silver at the temples, his eyes a brilliant green.

"What have we here?" he asked as he took a look at David, his voice as sharp and precise as a surgical tool. "A visitor this late? What do you want?"

"He says he's got info for you, Mr. A. but I don't think..."

"No, you don't think very well at all, do you Cavon? Why don't you let me do the thinking? I'm so much better at it."

The hood went into a sulky silence, and David took a closer look at the man who had made Shelley so unhappy.

Under any other circumstances, he would have enjoyed making him pay for things he'd done to her. But right now he knew that was impossible.

Suddenly he saw the movement again. A shadowy figure moved from behind a spiral staircase and slipped in behind the lifeboat. He knew it was Shelley, and he forced himself not to focus on where she was. She was dressed in black tights and a black sweater with a seaman's cap pulled down over her hair and most of her face. If either Armand or the Cavon creep turned his head, he would see her. David knew he had to work very hard to keep them interested in what he was doing so they wouldn't turn at all.

"I hear you're looking for a woman," he said quickly.

Armand gazed at him steadily, showing no emotion. "Who told you that?"

He produced the card once again. Armand took it from him and smiled a particularly oily smile.

"Well, you've heard wrong, my friend. I don't want the woman any longer." He flicked the card into the black water, and he turned back, his eyes glittering. "Now, all I want is the two children she has with her."

David knew what hearing that must do to Shelley's state of mind. Stay calm, Shelley, he urged silently. Just keep your head and get out of here. Think about this later, once you're safe.

"I've heard there's someone down south who knows something," he told Armand. "With the right incentive, I might be able to find out more."

He looked at Cavon in order to get Shelley in his peripheral vision again. She hadn't moved. *Run, get out of here, move.* Why wasn't she moving? He was urging her on with every fiber of his being. There was no telling how much longer he could keep these two men interested in what he had to say.

"How long will it take you to get the information?" Armand was asking.

David shrugged. "Twenty-four hours."

Armand shook his head. "Too long." His eyes shimmered with reflected light. "I tell you what. Why don't we go now, you and I, and get the information together?"

David shook his head slowly. "That won't work. My informant is unavailable, and he'll disappear altogether if you get involved." He shrugged, trying to remain calm. "I'll get back to you as soon as I can tomorrow, but that's the best I can do."

Cavon waved the gun again. "You want me to—?"

Armand gestured with his hand. "Put that away you Neanderthal. This gentleman and I are conducting business. Don't insult our friend." But when he turned back to David, his voice was cold as steel and rough with threat. "Listen, I want those kids. If you can pinpoint their location, I'll be extremely generous."

David licked his lips. This guy would as soon stab him in the back as smile at him. He was glad he wasn't really going to have to try to do business with him. There was no way to win with a snake like this. "How generous?" he asked.

Armand shrugged. "Two Gs. Is that good enough?"

No way. The guy was planning to cheat him, maybe even kill him, no doubt. Wary prickles slithered down his spine. All his survival instincts were telling him to get away as soon as he could. Still, he had to pretend to believe him.

He shrugged. "Sounds good."

He wondered how this was coming across to Shelley. Surely she knew that he'd seen her. A shadow was wavering on the boardwalk and relief sang through his veins. She'd made it. She was off the boat. Anything else from now on was gravy.

He had to give her time to get to the car. He hesitated, trying to think of something to prolong the conversation with, and Armand did it for him.

"I want to know who you are," he said acidly.

"Who, me?"

"Yes. Why is it that you talk like an American?"

"Because I am an American, Mr. A."

Armand nodded, though he didn't look convinced. "I know you don't want to reveal your source of information, and I can understand your reluctance, but just as evidence of good faith, tell me something of how you fit into things. What's your connection to the information?"

David thought fast. "I have a cousin who runs tourists down the coast." He shrugged. "He knows someone who got hired the other day. That's about it. I'll give you the rest when I know it."

"What's your cousin's name? Where does he live?"

David pretended outrage. "Why would I tell you? Then you'll give him the money."

Cavon laughed menacingly. "Hey, he's got a point there, boss."

Suddenly Armand had him by the lapels, gripping hard, his face a threatening mask. "I don't care who gets the money. I just want those kids. You *do* understand?"

David nodded rapidly, pretending more fear than he felt, but at the same time, controlling the urge to smash the creep in the face. "Sure. Sure. Don't worry. I won't let you down."

Armand let him go, and he straightened his shirt before turning to go. "I'll be back tomorrow. You won't be disappointed."

He started walking into the darkness. They didn't trust him any more than they should, and he knew they would tail him. He could feel them behind him, feel them watching, slipping from shadow to shadow. Then he heard a car start up. He glanced back but there were no headlights. They were just going to follow him in the dark, stick to him like glue until he revealed something to them. He had to think of a way to ditch them, but it wouldn't be easy with no wheels.

He walked faster, passing the end of the marina, turning down the street toward the fish market. Everything was closed and shuttered. It was late. There was no one else on the street.

At least Shelley had escaped. Hopefully she was already back at the café. He couldn't go back there now, not with them on his tail, but at least she was safe. The problem now was just to find a way to get back there without them knowing.

Suddenly a car came careering down a side street, straight for him, the headlights blinding him. He jumped aside, his heart in his throat, before he realized it was his own car. Shelley slowed as she came beside him and reached across to open the door.

"Get in," she yelled.

He rolled in, hitting the leather seat like a sack of cement, bruising his head and one shin in the process, yanking the door closed behind him, while she stepped on the gas, rocketing down the thoroughfare.

"Tell me what to do," she cried.

He'd lived in this town every summer of his life and he knew every alley, every side street. Shouting out quick directions, he guided her around in circles and through back streets until there was no telltale roar behind them any longer, no headlights. Then he led her to the beach, where they stashed the car in the jungle growth along the road and sat very still, catching their breath.

For a moment all that was heard was breathing. David took in one last, long breath and turned to her, grabbing her shoulders, shaking her hard.

"What the hell did you think you were doing?" he demanded through gritted teeth. "You could have been killed. He could have grabbed you..."

She threw her head back, her eyes closed. "You heard him," she replied calmly. "He doesn't want me. He wants Jill and Chris—"

His grip turned to a comforting caress. "Shelley..."

Her head came forward again, her eyes open and staring right into his. "I had to go. I couldn't just wait around for him to find me."

Her voice was crisp and without inflection. "I found this black sweater in a drawer. And the stocking cap was in the closet. My first thought had been to walk in and demand that Armand give me back my things, but I wore black, just in case, and when I got to the boat, my nerve failed. I knew I couldn't win face-to-face with him. He had all the firepower. So I decided my only hope was to be sneaky."

She paused for breath, but he didn't say anything. He let go of her and eased back into his seat, staring out into the silver black night, listening.

"I waited behind some boxes until there was no one in sight. I knew where the alarms were triggered and I avoided those spots when I jumped on board. And then I made my way around to the opening to Armand's cabin. I thought if he was out and I could get in there, maybe I could find my things and get away and it would be all over." She took a deep breath. "But he wasn't out. He was in his room with his girlfriend. I could see them through the glass in the door."

He turned back and touched her arm. "Shelley..."

She moved as though she were annoyed. "Do you think I care about that? I hate him, David. He makes my skin crawl. That's not the point. I was only angry because I knew I couldn't get my things with them in there. So I went into the room I'd stayed in, to see if he might have moved anything in there, but it was as clean as though no one had ever stayed there. My clothes had all been taken away. And then I went into the kids' room ... and ... and ..." Her voice began to shake. "It looked like they might be coming in from dinner at any moment."

He frowned, trying to understand why this upset her so much. "What do you mean?"

She put a hand to her forehead and steadied herself. "The beds were made. The covers were turned back. New stuffed animals were on the pillows. New clothes filled the closets." Her hand gripped his arm, the knuckles white. "David, he's so damn sure of himself."

He shook his head, denying. "He's just prepared."

"I was so stunned I just stood there, staring. Finally I kind of bumbled my way out onto the deck again. I thought they were going to catch me any minute. And then you showed up. You distracted them just enough for me to get off without them seeing."

He buried his hand in her hair. "Thank God," he said softly.

She turned to look at him, her eyes full of dread. "David, he's going to get them."

His other hand cupped her cheek. "No, Shelley. He's not."

She shook her head, her eyes deep as caverns. "When someone like that keeps after you and after you..." Her voice broke and she shook her head again. "No matter what I do, no matter where I go, if he wants to, he'll get them."

"No." He took her by the shoulders and tried to get through the wall of fear she was erecting. "He won't get them. We're not going to let him."

She blinked rapidly, clutching his arm with her fingers. "But, David, we're in a foreign country. If he gets hold of them, I'll never get them back."

He wanted to comfort her, to convince, to soothe her fears. "That's not going to happen, Shelley," he said earnestly. "Believe me. We're not going to let it happen."

She stared into his eyes as though she were trying to believe him. But she just couldn't do it.

She moved too quickly. He wasn't ready for it. In a fraction of a second she'd opened the car door and was twisting away from him, out of the car, running down into the white sand of the long, wide beach.

Pausing only to grab the keys out of the ignition, he was out of the car and running after her. Just a few feet short of the water he swooped her up into his arms and held her close.

"Shelley, Shelley," he breathed into her hair as she clung to him. "Don't you understand? You're not alone. It's not just you against him. I'm here. I'm with you. I'm not going to let anything happen. I swear to you. You and Jill and Chris are going to be safe."

She wanted to believe that as much as he wanted to convince her. Turning her face into his neck, she kissed him—short, quick kisses—again and again. He groaned, every part of him aware of her soft body, her delicious scent, her warm acceptance. He wanted her, but not only with the fast, hungry appetite of physical release. He wanted her with something deep and dark within him, something he'd never felt before and couldn't possibly understand right now.

He carried her back up the beach to where the jungle growth gave them some privacy, forming a protected cove.

Behind him the moonlight was silver on the liquid black of the sea. The hushed breeze from the ocean curled around them, tantalizingly spicy, exquisitely sultry. Golden sand crunched under his feet. And Shelley clung to him as though she would never let go.

Temptation was so strong, it choked in his throat. But he still could think, and he knew he had to stop this. He had to take her back to the car and drive her home and put her to bed with her children. He knew what he had to do, but he couldn't do it. He couldn't let go of her, couldn't warn her. His need was growing too powerful to resist.

Shelley's fingers sank into his hair, holding him prisoner to her warm mouth, and something deep inside him began to shudder with desire. The warmth of her mouth turned scalding as his tongue began to explore it, moving with sudden urgency as her fingers tightened on him, clutching him harder.

"David," she breathed into his open mouth. "David I need you...."

The sand was cool and somehow she was lying on it as David leaned over her, peeling away the sweater she had worn. His hand glided across the pale skin he'd uncovered, his fingers cupping breasts so soft they seemed to melt away at his touch. Her nipples were high and tight with desire. He yearned for her with every part of his being. There was no hope of restraint any longer. He couldn't deny her any more than he could stop breathing. It was beyond his control.

"I'm here, Shelley," he reassured her, his voice thick with passion, husky with his leashed need. "Shelley, are you sure?"

Her eyes opened wide and she stared into his as though she were looking straight into his soul. "Oh, yes, David," she sighed, half-laughing. "I'm sure. I'm very sure."

And that was good, because at this point he wasn't certain he would have been able to stop, anyway. He'd never felt such an overpowering drive before, never felt so completely out of control. He had to touch every part of her, had to feel her hard against him, had to know she was with him for this ride.

His hands weren't enough. He had to use his mouth, his lips, his tongue, tracing hot lines of hunger along her collarbone, around her navel, to the tips of her breasts.

She cried out and writhed beneath his stroking touch, her hips moving in the natural enticement of surrender. He tugged away the leggings and ran his hand up her thigh to where she was demanding contact with a fierceness that matched his own.

His stroke molded to her motion, burrowing into her warmth, and then his tongue took up the rhythm and she cried out, unable to wait any longer.

"Do you have something . . . ?" she murmured, her eyes glazed.

"I'll take care of it," he promised, though his hands were shaking so badly, for a moment he wasn't sure if he was going to be able to fulfill his pledge.

She reached for him, trying to guide him to where she needed him most, her urgency becoming a demand instead of a request, and he followed her lead, no longer thinking of holding back. Holding back would have been impossible.

The plunge took them both and she gasped when he entered, her eyes open and wild. He tried to hold her back, but it was too late. She drew him along, and he caught up with her, soothing her need. She cried out in wonder and relief, lifting her hips to take him deeper, harder, until they both crashed into the tempest that brewed inside them, hurling across the sky like lightning, feeling the thunder, feeling the eternity of space. They clung together to ride out the storm, until it left them breathing hard and glowing, lying tangled together in the sand.

He couldn't think. His mind wouldn't clear. And when he finally opened his eyes, it still took a few minutes to take in the full realization of just exactly what had happened.

"Shelley?" he murmured, turning his head to look at her. She was so close, her arms and legs still tangled with his. But all he saw were the tears in her eyes.

"Shelley." An agony of remorse swept through him, and he touched her face with his hand. "Oh, my God, did I hurt you?"

She smiled, her eyes brimming with liquid that caught the moonlight and made her look like an ethereal being. "You didn't hurt me," she whispered, putting her fingers to his lips. "It . . . it was just so . . . so . . ."

"I'm sorry, Shelley," he groaned, pulling back. "I shouldn't have . . ."

She grabbed his hair with both hands and yanked, hard. "Don't you dare say you're sorry," she demanded savagely, glaring into his eyes. "Don't you dare say it shouldn't have happened. This was one of the best things that has ever happened to me, and I won't let you belittle it."

He stared down at her, completely at sea. What on earth was she talking about? The tears were flowing from her eyes now, and he comforted her, but all the while he was stumped by her emotions, the way she'd reacted. He wanted to do something to make her stop crying, but in a strange way, he was beginning to suspect she was enjoying it.

Women. God knew he loved them. But what did they want?

Nine

***

"**I** want David to carry me." Chris's sleepy eyes barely opened a crack, but his little arms came up when David bent over him. "He's stronger."

Shelley glanced at David, suppressing a smile, wondering if he realized what an honor was being bestowed on him. Of all the men she'd ever gone out with, only Cubby had ever been accorded such trust by her son.

"Okay," she said softly, giving the little apartment one last look. "Jill, you can walk, can't you? I've got the suitcase. . . ."

"Why are you whispering?" David asked with a quick, slashing grin. "I don't think they can hear us down at the marina."

She threw him a look of pure exasperation. "We're sneaking off in the middle of the night, aren't we? We're supposed to whisper. It's in the rules of sneaking away."

"Ah." He nodded wisely. "I should have thought of that."

"Of course you should have. See how much better your life would be if you had a woman in it to explain these things to you?"

He turned with a startled look, but she refused to meet his gaze. "Come on, Jill," she said, urging along her sleepy daughter. "Let's go, honey. We want to get as far as we can before daylight."

Jill looked up at her, blinking, wincing from the light. "Where are we going?"

Shelley gave her a hug. "Home, sweetheart. We're going home."

Taking one last look around, David stepped out and locked the door from the outside, Chris clinging to his neck. The night was eerie, so quiet. The rest of the world was asleep. Shelley only hoped Armand was in bed, where he belonged. And all his thugs, with him. If they were prowling around the streets, their little sports car would be easy to spot heading out of town.

But she wouldn't think about that now. There was no other choice than to head for the border. What else could she do? She couldn't sit tight and wait for Armand to find her children. That was just plain unacceptable.

They all went down into the alley where David had parked the car to keep it out of sight from the street. The dinky trunk had barely enough room for the little suitcase. David threw some of his clothes in around it.

"Not exactly a family car, is it?" Shelley noted, squinting at the tiny back seat where her children were going to be spending many hours.

"Not many bachelors I know drive around in station wagons," David replied dryly.

She watched him as he settled the two children in the back, putting pillows under each sleepy head. Was he really so wedded to the concept of his bachelor image, or was he using it as a defensive measure? She couldn't help but grin at the thought.

They climbed into their respective bucket seats and Shelley looked at David and smiled. "Here we go," she said softly. Reaching out, she touched his hand. "Thank you, David. I'm really sorry to disrupt your life this way, but..."

He took her hand in his, squeezing it tightly. "I promised you I'd make sure you all were safe, Shelley," he told her, his eyes dark with earnest intent. "And that's exactly what I'm going to do."

Releasing her hand, he started the car. She sat back and watched Puerto Vallarta slip away. It had been barely an hour since they'd made love in the sand. If she closed her eyes, she could feel him again, feel her own incredible excitement. Was it the magic of the moment that had made it seem so intense, so infinitely more intimate than any experience she had ever had before? Was it something that could never happen again? Or would every time with David be that way?

She glanced at him, shivering slightly, wishing she knew how their lovemaking had affected him. She knew, deep inside, what it had done to her, though she wouldn't even allow herself to put it into words just yet. But she knew for sure that she would never be the same again.

In a way she'd placed herself in David's protection, and he'd given her his proof of commitment, all in those extraordinary few moments on the beach. The commitment was temporary. But so was her need. Still, not many people would have gone out of their way for her and her children like this. He was an exceptional man. If she wasn't careful, she might be able to convince herself that she was in love with him. It wouldn't be hard.

But it would be foolhardy. She knew he wasn't in the market for a long-term relationship. And neither was she, really. She had too much to prove—mostly to herself—before she could allow herself the luxury of loving. Armand was finally out of her life for good, and she wasn't about to jump right into someone else's arms. She had to stand on her own first.

"You'd better get some rest while you can," he told her softly. "In a few hours, you're going to have to drive so I can sleep."

She nodded and snuggled down into the seat. But her eyes kept drifting open and she kept looking at his profile. She wanted to hold him, to touch him, to bury her face in his chest. The yearning for contact swelled inside her. But it would be pretty silly to grab for him now, wouldn't it? So she forced herself to close her eyes again, and before long she was asleep.

The night was a dark tunnel he was driving through. There was no turning back. He felt like a lost soul running straight into hell.

He'd done exactly what he had sworn he wouldn't do, and now he was caught in the web, just as he'd known he would be. Shelley Brittman—the scent of her hair, the softness of her skin, the heat of her body, the curve of her breast in his hand, the passion he'd seen in her face—how was he going to get her out of his blood, now that she was in him? He was going to spend the rest of his life regretting what he'd done.

He glanced at the blond head on the seat beside him and almost laughed aloud at his own melodramatic ramblings. Regret it, hell. He could never regret it. Being close to this woman was probably going to turn out to be the high point of his life.

He sighed and forced himself to relax. He'd told her he would protect her from Armand and get her home as quickly as possible, and that was what he was going to do. He was committed. There was no question about it.

He'd had to close the café, of course. He'd explained everything to Rosa, and she would call his grandparents in the morning and explain to them. It was too bad, but he knew they would understand. If they'd been in town when all this had happened, they would have been the first to urge him to take her home.

The game plan was simply a mad rush for the border. He had some connections with federal employees in Mexicali, and he was pretty sure there would be no problem getting her a new tourist card in order to cross over to the U.S. If anyone gave them any flack, there was always the coyotes—he had a cousin who made his living that way.

His mouth twisted in grim irony. That would be something, wouldn't it? Shelley Brittman smuggling her way across the border with a bunch of illegals. Reed would have a good laugh.

Either that or kill him for letting his sister go through such an ordeal. It was hard to say which.

He'd hardly given Reed a thought in the past few days. Facing facts, he'd hardly given a thought to anything or anyone but Shelley ever since he'd been captivated by her tantalizing voice on the telephone. She'd filled his mind, filled his senses, and he knew she was addictive. He was going to have a hard time letting her go when he finally got her home.

Riding through the dark, he found it tempting to drift into fantasy. If only he could drive off in another direction and take Shelley and her two children with him to some other place, some other life, and never have to face reality again.

"David?" came Chris's childish voice from the back seat. "I have to go to the bathroom."

He laughed softly. Even here in the dark, reality was just waiting to slap him back to his senses.

"Okay, Chris," he said reassuringly. "We'll find a place."

The sun began to slant through the jungle growth a few hours later. They stopped to eat some breakfast rolls David had brought, letting the children run along the side of a stream. From where they sat, they could see pink flamingos wading in the shallow estuary and the ocean out in the distance.

"I wish we had time to explore the beach towns through here," Shelley said, leaning back and enjoying the view. "I've been in Mexico for over a week and yet I've hardly seen a thing."

"You'll see plenty on this trip. We've got a lot of driving ahead of us."

She looked at his serious face. He was making every effort to keep things businesslike today, as though he could somehow erase what had happened the night before. She suppressed a smile, but she couldn't help but tease him a little.

"But it's beaches I really want to see," she complained lightly. "I think I'll always have a special place in my heart for Mexican beaches."

He glanced at her quickly, caught the sparkle in her eyes, and only hesitated a moment before he reached out to pull her close. The children were out of earshot, and he risked a quick kiss on her willing mouth.

"You'd better behave," he told her softly, his eyes burning down into hers. "Or I'm going to have to take control again."

"Oh, is that what you call it?" She laughed up into his face.

He kissed her once more, harder this time, and the hunger rose in his gut like an ocean wave, strong and urgent, almost knocking him off his feet. If it hadn't been for the kids...

No, he told himself firmly as they got back into the car. This had to stop. The control he had to take was over himself.

They stopped for lunch in Mazatlan, and David indulged Shelley with a walk on the wide, white beach with the kids scampering around them, testing the water and racing back again. Jill stubbed her toe and ran right to David for comfort, while Shelley watched, bemused.

"You're really good with the kids, you know," she told him when Jill had run off again and they resumed their stroll.

He shrugged, shoving his hands down into his back pockets, and wouldn't meet her gaze.

"No, I really mean it. My children don't take to strangers very easily, but they've really taken to you." She glanced at him out of the corner of her eye. "I know you're not going to like this, but I'd say you were a natural-born father."

He seemed to shudder. "Hardly that."

She sighed, holding her hair back with one hand as the sea breezes tugged at it. She'd known a lot of men who seriously avoided commitment, but he took the cake. She wasn't sure if his position was something long and well thought out, or just a knee-jerk reaction, and she decided to put it to the test.

"You're not planning to get married, right?" she murmured idly.

"Right."

She turned to look at him. "Then you won't ever have any kids. You do realize that, don't you?"

No kids? Not ever? That set him back a bit. If anyone had asked him that question just days before, he would have happily answered, "No kids. Not ever." But that was before he knew any. Knowing Jill and Chris had changed his mind over how he felt about little ones, and suddenly the thought of never having any of his own was a real issue that he was going to have to come to terms with.

"Just why is it that you've never married?" she asked him abruptly, throwing caution to the wind.

For a moment she thought he was going to get angry, but when he turned and looked at her, his eyes were without emotion. "I'm happy, Shelley. I have a good business and well-rounded social life. And I don't see any reason to mess it up by taking chances with fate."

"I took those chances," she began.

"Yeah, and look where it got you."

She shook her head and pointed to the two towheads romping in the sandy water. "It got me Jill and Chris, David. I can never regret that."

He looked at them but he didn't smile. "I wouldn't want to bring children into the world and risk tearing them apart with a divorce," he admitted to her at last.

She nodded. That was exactly what she'd been afraid of. "I can understand feeling that way. But look at my kids, David. They've had tough times, sure, but they survived. They're pretty darn happy, if you ask me. And if you're going to say it would be better if they didn't exist . . ."

"No, of course not. You know how I feel about those kids."

Well, she didn't know, not really. But she was beginning to hope. She turned to him and smiled up into his face. "You need some kids of your own, David," she said softly. "I think it would do you good, and I bet you'd be happy."

Her smile faded and she studied his profile. "Don't you ever dream, David?" she asked softly.

"Dreams are for losers," he said roughly. "I have goals. I don't need dreams."

Chris called him from the water's edge and David's arm slipped away. She watched him go to her son, and she shook her head. She knew he was wrong. Dreams were the heart and soul of life. She only wished she had time to convince him of that.

The landscape changed as they drove on. The jungle gave way to desert and colorful agricultural tracts. There were mountains in the distance to the right and the ocean far to the left.

Jill and Chris were restless. Jill worked on her journal for a while, and Chris played the alphabet game, but neither of them could be satisfied with that forever. "How much farther?" was becoming a recurring refrain.

Shelley made them sing songs and then told them a story that put them right to sleep. Settling back down in her seat, she smiled at David and he grinned back.

"You know all the tricks, don't you?" he commented, admiring her more than he could express in words.

"I know a few," she admitted. "I've been doing this for quite a while, you know."

"And you like it," he observed.

"I do like it. I love being a mother." She stretched and put her head back, eyes half-closed. "But I'm about ready for some changes in my life."

He looked at her, a little startled. As far as he was concerned, she was perfect as she was. "What sort of changes?"

"Mostly small things." She turned and looked at him. "I feel as though a chapter of my life has closed now. Armand is finally gone."

"He's been gone for years, hasn't he?"

"Sure, in body. But it took this last week to really close that door. There are no lingering doubts about whether I did the right thing, whether I should have tried for a reconciliation for the children's sake, things like that. That is all over. I really feel as though I'm free to go on with my life now."

"Good. Just take it slow."

She sighed. "I don't know if I should take it slow. I feel as though I've been standing still for much too long, missing out, letting things pass me by. I want to run out and do all the things I've been avoiding for years."

He glanced at her. The sun splashed across her face like liquid gold. He wanted her. Every time he looked at her, he wanted her. He was beginning to feel as though his libido were running his nervous system. "Like what?"

"Like making my own living."

That was a concept he hadn't expected. "What?"

She turned in her seat, getting excited about her topic. "That's the thing that's going to change for sure. Here I've been telling myself I'd become so independent. But you know what? I've been kidding myself. I'm not independent at all. I still live in my parents' house. And to my eternal shame, when Armand crooked his little finger, I went running to him to see if he would like to take over my life for me again."

She paused, looking at him. "You know why I did that? Because I didn't trust in myself. I hadn't yet learned how to stand on my own. But I'm going to do that now."

He shifted uncomfortably in his seat, not sure he was going to like the new, self-reliant Shelley. "And just what are you going to do to effect this change?"

"First I'll go ahead with a project I've been thinking about for a while. A friend of mine has a business. She makes these huge floral arrangements for fancy restaurants and big weddings and receptions, things like that. She wants to expand, to add plant maintenance for businesses, but she needs a partner. I've decided that I'd like to go in with her."

Actually, why not? It sounded perfect for her. He could see her going in for consultations with her briefcase in her hand, her hair tied up in a conservative bun, glasses...even that turned him on. She couldn't do anything or dress in any way that would repulse him. Maybe he was obsessed. Or maybe he was just plain crazy. He shook his head, trying to get it cleared of all this romantic stuff, but it seemed to be a permanent condition.

"That sounds like a good idea," he said, rather reluctantly at first. Then he grinned, teasing her. "It wouldn't hurt you to find out how regular people live."

She shook her head and said softly, "David, I think I'm probably a lot more 'regular' than you want to believe."

His jaw tightened. That was the whole point here. She wasn't regular. She never could be. And he had to keep reminding himself of that fact before he did something really stupid.

All this talk about changing her life was probably mere musings, anyway. Why should she change? She had it great. She didn't have to do anything but indulge herself. She never had to worry about house payments, or whether or not she would be able to afford to send her kids to college. If they had a problem, she could hire a therapist for their every need. If she didn't like the weather, she could take off for Tahiti at a moment's notice. Who wouldn't want to live that way? And why would anyone give it up voluntarily? No, it didn't make a lot of sense. She was born to privilege, and she wouldn't know what to do without it. That was just the way things were.

"Then I'm going to get my own place," she was saying. "Somewhere in the suburbs, with a yard. And Jill and Chris can go to public school."

Right. Sure. "Just like regular kids," he said, trying to keep the sarcasm out of his voice.

"Exactly."

He glanced at her and said, a bit caustically, "You won't be a Brittman anymore."

She smiled and threw her arms out. "I'll always be a Brittman. I can't deny that. But I can be...I don't know. More of a real woman."

His eyes smoldered as he looked at her. "You are a real woman," he said firmly. Any more real, and he would be a dead man right now.

She laughed softly, touching his cheek with her hand, brushing back the dark hair that had fallen over his forehead. "To you, maybe I am. Now I just have to convince myself."

He gritted his teeth, not responding. It was insane how much he loved it when she touched him like that. In some ways he would miss that most of all. That, and her voice that still sent chills down his spine. How could he grow so used to her in such a short time? His life was going to seem empty without her. The dread was already starting like an ache in the bottom of his stomach. He wanted to pull over to the side of the road and make wild love to her, just to blot out the threatening pain. But he had to content himself with glancing at her, taking in how lovely her face looked as she gazed out the window, how firmly her breasts stood out against the blue cotton of his sweater that she was wearing, how her long fingers curved gracefully against the black leggings.

He wanted to make her talk again, just so he could listen to her voice. "Tell me a story, Shelley," he said quietly, mimicking the kids, and she laughed, not realizing he was speaking in deadly earnest.

The late-afternoon sun was blinding him as it burned through the windshield. But that wasn't the worst of it. The car was losing speed, and the engine was beginning to sputter.

"What's that funny noise?" Shelley asked.

"My car is dying." He gave her a weary smile as he pulled over to the side of the empty road. "Stand by for an autopsy report."

She got out with him, leaning in over the engine and watching him poke and prod, until he asked her to get in and try to start the engine for him. Then there was more poking and a few swear words. She had no idea what he was doing, but she had absolute faith in him.

"Well, that's that," he said at last, wiping his hands on a rag she handed him.

"That's what?"

"We're stuck. It's the carburetor. It's going to take me at least overnight to fix this thing. We're going to have to find a place to stay."

A place to stay? But that was impossible. They were making a run for home and safety. Pure panic rose in her. Suddenly she was sure Armand was about to come over the crest of the last hill at any moment. "But we have to keep going," she said, grabbing David's sleeve. "We've got to get across that border."

Turning, he touched her face. "Shelley, we can't go any farther. This is it. We're stuck until I get this car moving again."

She put one hand to her forehead, her eyes a little wild. Her imagination was sending up images of her children being driven off in the back of a long, black car, waving at her out the back window. "Can't we call a tow truck or something?"

"Not out here in the middle of nowhere."

He was right, of course. She forced herself to calm down. If Armand were following them, he surely would have caught up to them by now. In the meantime, she had to think of her children. They needed someplace to stay.

David was back under the hood. She put a hand out to shield her eyes from the sun and looked up and down the desolate highway. Suddenly she caught sight of something.

"Look, David," she called, excited. "There, off the main road to the right, down that hill. Isn't that a little motel or something?"

It was, and it was mostly downhill to get there.

"Help me push," David said. "You go to the back of the car, I'll steer and push from the side. We can roll it right into the parking lot."

Pushing a car along the highway was a new experience for Shelley, but she didn't do badly. The only problem was, as they neared the ramshackle collection of cabins and cottages, they began to have second thoughts.

"This place reminds me of a certain spooky motel in a certain very scary movie," she called out to David from behind the car as they came toward it.

He paused, panting for a moment, wiping sweat from his brow. "It's not going to be the world-class accommodations you're used to," he told her. "But it'll be okay."

Still, he saw what she meant as he took another look at the place. All it needed was a big house on a hill with a rocking chair in the window....

"Let's just get it up to the entryway. Then I'll go in and see if they have room for us."

Shelley made a face, but she didn't show it to him. It was too bad the car was too small to sleep in. Jill was leaning out the window, looking excited.

"Wow," she said. "Looks neat."

Neat was the last thing it looked. Shelley bit her lip and forced back the sardonic comments struggling to break free from her sealed lips. She was not going to act like a spoiled rich girl. She could rough it with the best of them—or the worst of them, as the case might be. At least she would make every attempt. She refused to let David sneer at her.

He was walking back to say something. "I'm going to sign in under my name," he said, looking as though he expected a reaction from her.

She blinked at him, not certain what he was driving at. "Sure."

"I mean, I'm going to say we're married."

"Oh." She wanted to laugh. It was bubbling up her throat. Did he think she would object? Hardly. He was the one who ran from wedlock.

"Better warn the kids you're adopting them for the night," she said, her eyes dancing.

He nodded and stuck his head in the window. "I'm checking us into this motel as one family," he told them. "Just remember, if anyone asks you, your last name is Coronado. Okay?"

Jill giggled. Chris shrugged. Coronado, Alexiakis, Brittman, it was all the same to him.

But Shelley said it out loud, rolling it around on her tongue. "Mr. and Mrs. David Coronado." Her smile was faint and didn't reflect the growing warmth she felt inside. "Gee, that sounds like fun."

His dark look was almost a glare. "You've got a funny idea of fun, lady."

Pretending mock horror, she put a hand to her mouth. "Oh, that's right. I forgot I was talking to Mr. Perpetual Bachelor."

"Damn right."

But he was grinning, too, as he went back to the open door of the car and bent to finish their job of pushing. She leaned her shoulder into the task again. In a few minutes they would be at the motel, and she would be able to shower and rest. And the two of them would have one more evening together. That was a cheering thought. Maybe this wouldn't turn out to be such a disaster after all.

Ten

***

"I don't know, Shelley," David said, looking back, as they maneuvered the little car right up to the entrance of the motel park. "Another black-and-white movie from the Fifties comes to mind, now that I really get a good look at the situation."

Shelley stopped and looked toward where he was staring.

"What on earth . . . ?" She took a step nearer and gaped at the yard full of powerful, low-slung motorcycles. They were everywhere, brightly painted, gleaming with chrome.

Moving forward, she clutched his arm. "David, we've got to go someplace else. This motel has been taken over by a motorcycle gang."

He nodded, fascinated by the various machines assembled before them. "That's what it looks like."

She glanced at his face. He wasn't getting it. This wasn't good, this was bad. Biker types weren't the sort one wanted to fool around with. She'd seen all the movies, read all the thriller fiction. Motorcycle gangs were bad news.

"We've got to get out of here," she urged, tugging on his arm. "You know what these people do to lonely, stranded motorists? They eat them alive."

"You don't say, sweetheart," said a booming voice from just behind her. "It's a scandal, ain't it?"

Gasping, she whirled to find herself confronting a large woman in worn black leather with a large gold ring through her right nostril, standing with her arms akimbo, staring at them. At least, Shelley thought the woman was staring at them. She was definitely staring somewhere in their general direction. With those huge reflector sunglasses on, and the sun beating down, it was hard to tell for sure just where.

"Uh, hi," Shelley said weakly, backing up against the car.

"Hi, yourself," the large woman roared, stepping closer, looking large as a house. "Now what's this about our eating habits?"

David stepped between them, choking with laughter. "I'm David Coronado," he said, holding out his hand. "You'll have to forgive Shelley. She doesn't get out much. And even worse, she believes what she sees on TV."

The large woman hesitated only a moment before taking his hand in her beefy version. "Pleased to meet you, David," she said. "I'm Marge. And I never watch TV."

"That's wise of you." He gestured toward the sea of motorcycles. "These are some great bikes. I see a couple of real vintage beauties in there." He pointed toward one sleek, black model. "I used to have a Hog a lot like that one in my younger, wilder days."

Marge laughed and slapped him on the back, nearly sending him face-first into the dust. "Honey, I may not be any younger, but I get wilder all the time. You should try it yourself."

Shelley watched as they discussed sidecars and fuel tank shapes, and then the carburetor problems he was having with the car. She kept her breathing steady, watching for a chance to grab David so that they could escape from this place, and especially from this motorcycle mama. Shelley had children to protect, for heaven's sake—two children who were staring out the window at Marge, fascinated by her bizarre appearance.

"So you folks are planning to stay here?" Marge said at last. "Great. Tell you what—" reaching out with her gloved hand, she took Shelley's arm "—I'll take your lady in to the office and help her get signed up."

Shelley shrank from her, looking quickly at David for salvation, making significant faces and shaking her head. "Oh no, I don't think..."

But David seemed to have gone blind and deaf. "That would be great," he was saying, grinning at her. "Thanks, Marge. I want to get this car parked somewhere I can work on it, and then I'll bring the kids on in."

"But, David—"

"Go with Marge. She'll take care of you."

That was just what she was afraid of. Before she had a chance to get another word in, she found herself being dragged toward the lobby, such as it was, sputtering but unable to get any sympathy from either party.

"Hey, Gertie," Marge yelled as they came in the door. "I got a customer for you. She needs a double, 'cuz she's got two kids with her."

Gertie was a wizened lady who looked as though she'd been baking her skin in the sun for so many years, she'd dried up like a twig. She shuffled out from a back room, looked Shelley over and shook her head.

"Sorry. We're all booked up."

Relief spilled through Shelley. "Oh, gee, that's really too bad. I guess I'd better go tell David."

She pulled out of Marge's grasp and started to turn for the door, but Marge grabbed her again, spinning her back.

"Hey, not so fast. Listen up, Gertie. You just go ahead and give these nice people the room me and Charlie've been in all week. They only need the place for one night. We can bunk with Mad Dog Crank. He's got plenty of room."

Shelley paled. The concept of using Marge's room boggled her mind. The fact that there was a person staying in this motel going by the name of Mad Dog nearly did her in. "No, no, we couldn't . . ."

"Sure you could." Marge beamed. "Hell, we'd love to do it for you."

David came in just in time to second the motion. Shelley was caught, and she tried to smile. Before she had a chance to take a stand, she found herself being dragged by Marge toward the rustic cabin where they were going to be spending the night.

"We're a motorcycle club, honey, not a gang," Marge told her sternly. "We're the Lancers, based north of San Francisco. We come down here every year for a little wienie roast. Know what I mean? This motel is our favorite. Always has been."

She threw open the door of the cabin, and Shelley took a tentative step inside, then stopped. There was a man sitting in the gloom.

"Meet Charlie, my hubby." Marge bustled in, whipping off her sunglasses and revealing a pair of lovely violet eyes with the longest lashes Shelley had ever seen. "This is Shelley. She and her guy, David, they broke down and need a place to lay their heads for the night. So we're moving in with Mad Dog Crank."

Charlie looked up from his reading. He had large, kind eyes and a professorial beard. He nodded, rising from his chair. "How do you do?" he asked formally, shaking hands. "It's nice to meet you."

"I'll go tell Mad Dog," Marge said breezily. "You can get started moving in, honey." And she was out the door again.

Shelley swallowed and smiled at Charlie. She was still reeling from the overpowering influence of the woman.

"You...you're married to Marge?" It was definitely hard to believe.

"I certainly am." He smiled and offered her a seat. She sat down on the edge, fidgeting.

"But you don't seem like—" She stopped, embarrassed.

"Like I'm the sort to belong in a motorcycle club?" He smiled. "I'm not. And I don't. Marge belongs to the Lancers, not I. I teach philosophy to undergraduates at Amber University in Marin County."

Shelley blinked. "Oh," she said in a very small voice.

He laughed at her obvious confusion. "Marge and I have been married for fourteen years. We have two boys at home. We only do this once a year, coming down to Mexico with her friends. It's great fun. It's a change of scene from the university library and those boring faculty meetings."

Shelley shook her head. He seemed like such a nice man, the sort she might have met at a benefit for the opera or at an alumni meeting. "I've heard of opposites attracting, but this is—" She shrugged.

"Ridiculous?" He smiled. "But it's not, you see. Though we do have definite differences, they only add spice and interest to a relationship based on very similar values and goals in life. I'd venture to say we have more to talk about with each other than most couples our age. And she does a great job keeping our cars in tune."

He laughed and Shelley laughed right along with him, not sure if her head had stopped spinning yet. "I'm sorry, but I just can't imagine what your faculty dinners must be like."

"Marge doesn't wear the nose ring, or her leathers, but otherwise, she's pretty much herself. And once people get to know Marge, they usually love her."

Shelley nodded. She was just beginning to realize that. This strange couple was giving her a whole new perspective. "I can hardly wait until David meets you," she said suddenly, biting her lip, her eyes sparkling. "Promise me you'll tell him all the things you've told me."

Marge and Charlie moved out cheerfully, and Shelley and the children moved in. The cabin was roomier and homier than she'd expected, with a bedroom and a couch in the living room that pulled out into a bed, and a sink, burner and small refrigerator. Jill picked some wildflowers and put them in a vase, and Shelley opened all the windows to let the afternoon sun in. As she worked to make things cozy, she indulged herself in a casual fantasy about what it would be like to keep house for David.

"Hey, this isn't half bad," he commented when he came in to clean up from working on the car.

A simple comment, but it warmed Shelley's heart.

Mad Dog, it turned out, was a marvelous mechanic. He found the problem with the carburetor and the men were well on the way to fixing what could be taken care of without parts. Meanwhile, Jill and Chris were making friends with some of the bikers' children, and having a wonderful time in the courtyard, sitting on the motorcycles and making engine noises.

Shelley watched and laughed. Marge introduced her to some of the other women, and soon what had begun as a disaster turned into a pleasant holiday. But Shelley found her gaze constantly straying to where David was leaning over the engine of the car. For some reason she enjoyed looking at him, at the way his hair fell over his forehead, the way his hands moved gracefully as they worked, the look of complete concentration on his handsome face, the bulge of his biceps as they swelled beneath the sleeves of the T-shirt. And every time she looked at him, her heart beat a little faster, and prickles of wariness scattered across her skin. Was she getting in too deep? Only time would tell.

As evening approached, David came into the cabin and took a long, hot shower and cleaned off every bit of grease he could find. The car was virtually ready. They could leave tonight, if he pushed it. But he didn't want to. He'd feel better if they left in the morning—in case anything happened again. He'd hate to be stranded with the kids out in the middle of nowhere, in the middle of the night.

He towel dried his hair and dressed in fresh clothes, taking his time. He could hear Shelley humming in the next room as she puttered about, and he smiled. She even hummed sexy.

This would be their last night together.

His smile faded. He didn't want to think about that. He opened the door and stepped out into the room, and Shelley turned and smiled.

"Marge just stopped by and invited us to their campfire dinner tonight," she told him. "I guess they all get together and barbecue food. I said we'd love to come, since I don't see any sign of a restaurant anywhere near here. So I guess it's either that or starve."

"That's fine." He glanced from one room to the other. "One bed and a couch?" he asked.

"Yes." She looked at him steadily, her blue eyes dark. "How shall we set up the sleeping arrangements?" she asked in a quiet voice.

He looked at her, hesitating, his eyes questioning hers, searching for cues. "I don't know. What do you think?"

Her gaze clung to his, electric with possibilities. "Two beds," she said with absolutely no inflection. "Four people."

He looked at the double bed and swallowed. He could already feel the cool sheets, feel her warm body against his. But he turned and muttered, "I don't know. I guess we could do the same thing we've been doing—you and the kids in the bed, me on the couch." He looked the question at her again.

She smiled, her eyes luminous. "It opens up into a bed," she said softly. "There's plenty of room for two."

His heart was beating like a piston in an engine and he took a step toward her, ready to take her in his arms right now. But he couldn't do that. Stopping, he took a deep breath and turned toward the doorway.

He looked back at her over his shoulder, not sure why he was so reluctant to come right out and say what he wanted, what he knew they both wanted. "Whatever you think," he muttered, and then he was out the door, escaping decisions.

The Lancers were already gathering for their nightly campfire, and he mingled, talking about bikes with one person after another. But when Shelley came out of the cabin in a white dress Marge had borrowed for her from one of the other women, he was suddenly very thirsty and had to get himself a beer and drink it down. Lord, she was beautiful, with the white fabric swishing about her knees and the pink flower pinned to hold back her silver hair. He could feel the stir going through the other men as she came among them and they got a look at her. But her eyes were looking through the crowd, searching for him. He pulled himself to his feet so she could see him, and he saw the way her face lit up when she caught sight of where he was. She smiled, and something swelled inside him, part pride, part anguish. She was his—for tonight.

The food was great—barbecued ribs and baked potatoes. David sat with Shelley to eat, with Jill and Chris at their feet, but soon they were separated again as the crowd milled about them. He felt an elbow in his ribs and looked around to find Marge grinning at him.

"Here's my advice to you, kiddo. Marry the gal."

"Marry her?"

"Sure. She was a little stiff at first, but once you get to know her, she's all right. And you can see by the way she looks at you, she's head over heels."

"No." He shook his head, ready to contradict her. Didn't she see the problem here?

But Marge was not easily contradicted. "Sure," she insisted. "She's crazy about ya."

David grinned, shaking his head. Marge was obviously a romantic biker. "How did you know we weren't married already?"

She grunted. "Nobody who's married makes cow eyes like the two of you do. You can't fool old Marge, honey." She sobered, frowning at him. "But listen. I really mean it. Don't let this one slip away. When you find that one in the world for you, you better grab on while you have the chance."

David's smile faded and he looked at the woman, wondering if she might really have the answers. "But what's the use if you know it won't work out?"

Marge shrugged grandly. "Anything can work out if you really want it to. If you're willing to go halfway, she'll go the other. Take my word for it." She slapped him on the back. "Look at me and Charlie." She laughed, then sobered and told him seriously, "And if you're not prepared to take the chance, then you don't deserve love, anyway."

She gave him another of her signature back slaps and moved on, shouting orders to the women who were bringing out the cake and ice cream. David watched her go. Her advice was probably good for some people, but she didn't know all the facts. There was more to love than just grabbing something because it was good. There were consequences to think about and guard against. He knew that only too well.

After the food had been consumed, they sat around the fire and sang old songs. Shelley sat beside him, her long hair like spun gold in the campfire light. They laughed together at the silly jokes, and her slender hand slid into his. Holding hands in the dark. He felt like a teenager again, shy and confident at the same time.

Charlie brought out his guitar, another man had a harmonica, and the group launched into a retrospective of every folk song the fifties produced. The adults were having a ball, but the children were drooping. David was joining in the chorus of an old spiritual when Chris wandered over and sank into his lap. So naturally, his arms went around the little boy. He held him close without a second thought as he continued singing. The young head rested against his chest, and in moments, Chris was sound asleep.

David looked down, amazed at the protective feeling that overwhelmed him, amazed at how good it felt to hold a child. Chris was so young and so trusting. He wanted to hold him tightly, to make sure nothing ever hurt him.

Looking up, he met Shelley's eyes and found them brimming with tears. She leaned forward and kissed him softly on the lips, then turned away to wipe her eyes. He waited for the trapped feeling to rise in his chest, but it didn't come. And when Jill arrived a few minutes later, looking for a place to settle, he made room for her on the other side of his lap. Then he held them both and felt as though he were drowning in an emotion he couldn't name or turn away from, and he didn't dare look at Shelley at all.

"We'd better put them down," Shelley whispered at last.

He nodded, though he was strangely reluctant to give them up. Shelley took Chris from him and they said goodnight to the others before carrying the two children into the cabin.

Shelley had already made up the couch into a double bed. She laid Chris down and turned to help David settle Jill under the covers. Neither of them came right out and said it, but they both knew what the plan was, and when Shelley turned and went into the bedroom, David followed her.

She turned and smiled at him. "One last night," she said softly. "I guess that's all we have."

He reached out and ran his fingers through her silvery hair. Yes, it was all they had. Very soon, every excuse for their being together would be exhausted, and they would probably never see each other again. It wasn't as though they ran with the same crowd in good old San Diego, or lived in the same neighborhood. The wildlife parading through his backyard was more likely to be gophers than polo ponies.

"Why do you have to be so beautiful?" he breathed as he pulled her toward him.

She laughed softly, reaching to touch his face with the palm of her hand. "Don't you dare charge this one on me, mister. There's enough blame here for both of us."

She was right. It wasn't her. It was him. He'd only had to hear her voice that first day on the telephone and he was a goner before the receiver had settled back down in its cradle. And now he was trapped, tangled in emotions he couldn't control, needing her like he needed air to breathe.

He held her face in his hands and looked into it, searching for an answer to the question that burned inside him, despite all his efforts to suppress it. Did she feel it too, this connection between them?

He knew she felt passion. He knew she liked him. But did she feel the pull the way he did? As though something primeval had reached out and wound its chains around his heart, binding him to her in ways he couldn't begin to comprehend.

But staring into her eyes was like wandering through ice caverns that sparkled with light. It was lovely and exciting and welcoming, but it was also similar to losing oneself in a maze. There were no answers there, none that he could see.

Or maybe he just didn't know how to read them.

He combed his fingers back into her hair, his eyes narrowing as he studied the line of her cheek, the curve of her ear, the feathery arch of her eyebrow. She was truly a work of art.

"Tell me pretty things, David," she said at last, and suddenly that haunted look was back in her eyes. Her hands flattened against his chest and she looked into his gaze longingly. "Tell me that everything is going to be all right, that you like my perfume, that this is more than physical."

He wanted to tell her that he loved her. He knew that was what she was asking, but how could he lie to her? He didn't love her. He didn't know how to love a woman, not the way she wanted to hear it.

Pushing the hair away from her ear, he dropped small kisses beside it, rubbing his face against hers. "Making love with you is like a prayer, Shelley," he whispered, drinking in the scent of her hair. "It's a tribute we make to the sun god."

She laughed low in her throat, letting her head fall back so he could press his lips to her throat. "You crazy Aztec," she murmured. "I'd better watch out or you'll take my heart as a sacrifice."

He pulled back and explored her gaze again, searching the maze for her real meaning, but she was smiling and her fingers began to work on the buttons of his shirt, releasing them one by one.

He found the zipper at the back of the white dress. Pulling it open loosened the bodice so that it slipped down, almost freeing her breasts. His hands did the rest, and his breath choked in his throat as he looked at her.

His mouth took hers slowly, softly, moving with exquisite patience. They had all the time in the world, and this once he meant to treat her as she deserved to be treated. She opened to him as though she'd just been awakened to the possibilities he had in store, exploring him with wonder in her touch. Her touch was hypnotic and her mouth was intoxicating. She tasted like brandy, hot and smooth and exciting, and he was drunk from the very first sip.

He leaned her back onto the bed without releasing her mouth from the control of his own. She arched beneath him as they fell back, and his hands pushed the dress down to her waist. Her breasts felt full and round beneath him, burning into his chest with their tantalizing eroticism. He trailed kisses down her neck and her chest, until he had captured one nipple in his mouth, and then he tugged slowly, as though he were moving in water, as though he had to savor every nuance of sensation and give it all back to her.

She moaned softly, digging her fingers into his hair, and her body moved. He tugged the dress down and away, and did the same with the filmy bit of nylon she wore beneath it. She was naked now, long and slender, a symphony of curves and angles that made him see stars as he looked at her. How could such beauty be real? And what a miracle that it could be his.

He ran his hand down across her stomach and cupped her warmth, stroking softly, slow and easy, like a dance, like the waltz, swaying back and forth, creating a song, creating a dream, splashing pastel colors across the sky.

"David," she murmured, her breath coming more quickly. "Don't take too long, I can't stand it....."

But she loved it, and he knew it. Pulling back, he looked at her again, all cream and shadows in the light of the small bedside lamp, all hills and valleys, like the desert landscape in the late afternoon, sunlight turning it golden, shadows hiding mysteries.

For the first time in his life, he understood poetry. A woman's body was eternal, the wellspring of life, as close to nature as he would ever get. Something surged inside him, overwhelming him. He touched her with a reverence that didn't erase the hunger he felt to have her. It was all part of one whole. She was eternity. She was destiny. She was fulfillment. She was everything he could ever dream of having. She was love.

Her hands slid down under his belt, and he loosened it and let her push away his clothes, turning so she could touch him, mold him, forcing his mind and body to be still, even while he felt an urgency that was building to a crest.

Her breath was coming in short gasps, and he knew it was time. He spread her legs and entered, planning to hold back a little longer, planning to build to a slow, steady rhythm. But she couldn't wait any longer. She cried out, her fingers digging into his back, pulling him tighter and harder, and as she leapt into the dance, she carried him along, taking him higher and higher, until his vision went white and he was sure they'd found their way to heaven.

"Times like this I wish I still smoked," he muttered, pushing himself up to lean against the headboard.

She laughed, pulling the sheet around herself as she sat up, cross-legged, on the bed. Have I told you lately that I love you? she thought as she looked at him. There was no getting around it. That was just the way things were.

But things weren't supposed to be that way. She wasn't ready for a new relationship. She'd been telling herself that for years now—so it must be true—mustn't it?

"Since we don't smoke, how about some ice cream?" she suggested, reaching for his shirt and slipping into it before she got up. "I saw some in the little refrigerator. Mint chip."

He smiled at her. "Okay. Just a little."

She dropped a kiss on the top of his head and went out to get it, tiptoeing past the sleeping children and getting two dishes from the shelf over the sink. Her heart was full of feeling for him. She felt like dancing. And still, while her body and soul were celebrating, her head was in the doldrums. She wasn't supposed to be doing this.

But maybe it was time for a reassessment. As she spooned out the mint green ice cream, she went over things in her mind, getting it straight. She wanted to be in love. It felt good. And it felt right, despite the way it ought to feel. What exactly had she been telling herself? She was almost thirty, and yet she was convinced that it was too soon to take a chance? That she was not ready? That the timing was bad? She wasn't allowed to reach for the brass ring because she hadn't worn the right party dress? What was she, crazy?

No other man had ever made her laugh the way David did. No other man had ever treated her children so well. No other man had ever made her heart race just by looking at her a certain way. And no other man had ever made love to her the way he did. But she was supposed to give him up because of timing?

That was what was crazy. And she wasn't going to be tyrannized by thinking like that anymore.

So it was official. She was in love. Admitting that to herself made her feel as though her skin was glowing. She was in love.

Now the problem was going to be to get him to join in the fun.

She went back with the ice cream and handed him his bowl.

"Take off the shirt," he said solemnly, his eyes very dark.

"Why?"

"Because I like you better without it."

Grinning, she did a little strip tease and plopped back down on the bed, pulling the sheet up to cover strategic areas and taking a spoonful of ice cream onto her tongue. They ate in silence for a moment, Shelley watching him, thinking hard. And then she asked her first question.

"David, will you ever get married?" she said, looking at him and shaking her head, pretending it was a casual inquiry.

He refused to meet her gaze, staring at the ceiling. "Probably not."

"Why not?" She leaned forward on one arm. "What scares you so?"

He looked shocked at the very concept. "Who said I was scared? I'm not scared, just smart." He shifted, pulling part of the sheet over himself as though he had to hide that, too, now that she was delving into private matters, and went back to eating his ice cream. "I saw what can happen to a marriage. My parents loved each other as much as anyone, but it still didn't work out."

She pursed her lips, twirling her spoon through the cold confection. This was going to be a tough nut to crack. "Why do you think that was?" she mused, watching his eyes for his reaction.

He shrugged. "Probably because they came from such different backgrounds." He glanced at her. "My father was a blue-collar immigrant. My mother was a school teacher. They were from different countries, different traditions."

His face softened, remembering. "But you should have seen how they looked at each other. Whenever they were together you could see it in their eyes, the way they touched each other." His eyes darkened. "Still, they couldn't make it together. What they wanted out of life, what they were willing to put up with to get what they wanted, were just too dissimilar to exist side-by-side. God knows they tried. They tried for twelve years. But it didn't work. And no matter what they did they were miserable apart." He grimaced, setting aside his empty bowl. "And they were miserable together. Neither one of them could adjust."

"That's the key, isn't it?" She pounced upon the idea. "Adjustment. If you found a woman you could 'adjust' to, do you think you might get married?"

He flashed her a quick grin. "I won't be the one adjusting. She will."

"Oh, right!" She threw a pillow at him, starting a quick wrestling match that ended up with some rather personal tickling.

"But all in all," she went on when the wrestling wound down, picking up the thread from where they'd left it and at the same time cleaning up her spilled ice cream and setting the bowl on the floor. "Don't you think your parents were lucky?"

Obviously he didn't think so at all. "Lucky? How?"

"They had love. Even if they couldn't make it work. They had something special between them, and I'm sure they had many, many wonderful times together."

"Big deal. They also had a lot of misery."

Shelley frowned. Why had she ever thought she could do this? How did you change someone who didn't want to change?

"And anyway," he went on, evidently feeling he was making his points brilliantly. "After the horrible experience you've had, what gives you an excuse for being optimistic about marriage?"

Shelley shook her head, denying everything. "I can't blame my disaster on the institution of marriage. I blame it on the man I picked."

"But that's just it. How do you ever know if you're picking right?"

"You don't. You have to do what you have to do. And lots of times it's wrong." She shrugged. "That's what divorce is for."

He shook his head, his mouth twisted. "You don't ever *have* to get married."

She pulled the sheet up tightly against her chest and slid over next to him against the headboard. She was going to have to bare her soul, and she didn't want to have to look him in the eye when she did it.

"It depends on how you define things, I guess," she said lightly. "For instance, I married Armand because I had to at the time."

He glanced at her. "What do you mean, you had to?"

"Because of where I was emotionally." She took a deep breath and squared her shoulders. "I needed him. I needed to marry someone who had his standing."

He moved impatiently. "So you married a sleazy crook like that for status?"

"A sleazy crook wasn't what I married, David. He was respected in social circles in those days. I needed his respect, his image, for legitimacy. Don't you see that? I wasn't a rebellious girl in any way. I wanted in, not out. And I was on the ragged edge, because I'd been branded as being a flake. At that time, I couldn't have married anyone—'' She paused, closing her eyes. Here came the hard part. But she had to be honest. Anything else would be lying. ''I couldn't have married anyone, say, like you. In order to marry someone like you, I would have had to have had the self esteem necessary to tell them all to take a flying leap. And I didn't have that then.''

He sat very still, not moving, not looking at her. ''Do you have it now?''

''Yes.'' Her answer left no room for doubt, but she wasn't sure it was what he wanted to hear at all.

He'd shifted, turned so that he could look at her face, and his eyes were cold with outrage. ''What kind of stupid society do you come from, where a crook like Armand is accepted, and an honest, hard-working person like me is shunned?'' he demanded, his voice clipped and angry.

She wasn't sure if she'd done the right thing telling him, but she couldn't back down now. Putting a hand on his arm, she tried to make him understand. ''David, please, we're not talking substance here. We're talking imagery. We're talking superficial things that don't last. Just like my marriage didn't last, because that was exactly what it was based on.''

He was quiet for a long moment, digesting what she'd said, and she began to relax. He was a smart guy. He could figure it out for himself. He knew she wasn't that insecure girl any longer. She didn't need that sort of reassurance, and she didn't need to be part of that social scene. She'd learned how sterile it really was. She didn't think she had to explain it to him.

Finally he turned to her with a crooked smile. ''So, do you think you'll get married again?''

Relief flooded her. He got it. ''Me? Possibly.''

His eyes were hooded. "What kind of man do you think you'll marry?"

She tilted her nose in the air. "Someone I love."

He gave a short laugh. "Didn't you try that last time?"

She snuggled closer to him. "I plan to try it again."

His eyes darkened and he reached out to take her hand in his. "To the race car driver?" he asked softly.

She bit back a grin. "I don't think so."

He was quiet for another minute before he said, "You went to France with him."

"Yes, David. I went to France with him." She squeezed his hand and grinned up into his face. "His sister was one of my best friends in school in England. The three of us stayed together in a lovely hotel suite big enough to house the Royal Guard. Big deal."

He stared into her eyes with such intensity she almost felt scalded. "You weren't having an affair with him?"

Reaching out, she touched his cheek. "How could I have an affair with him?" she murmured softly. "I was saving myself for you."

She only half meant it as a joke. He kissed her, and the sheet fell away and their bodies came together, too warm, too real to resist. She wished she knew something special she could do to make him feel the sort of pleasure he gave her. But maybe that wasn't necessary. Maybe he already did.

Eleven

They were on the road early the next morning, after waving goodbye to the Lancers and Marge and Charlie. Marge packed all sorts of cookies and cakes for the kids to take along, so at least they wouldn't starve if they broke down somewhere in the desert. Jill and Chris waved and waved until they couldn't see anyone out the back window any longer.

"They turned out to be the nicest people," Shelley said, settling down in the passenger's seat. "I don't know when I've had more fun."

"That'll teach you not to stereotype," David told her smugly. "You thought they were going to be hoods because they ride motorcycles, and instead, they're just like anyone else."

"I guess I learned my lesson," Shelley said in a silly voice. Then she sobered. "But what about you, David? What's it going to take to teach you not to stereotype me?"

His eyes widened. "What are you talking about?"

"You know very well what I'm talking about. Stop making assumptions about me and what I need just because of my background. It *ain't* necessarily so, you know."

She turned back to see how the kids were doing, and David frowned into the morning sun. He knew what she meant, but that didn't mean he agreed with her point. She was who she was—there was no getting around it.

And last night who she'd been had been something out of this world. He'd never made love to a woman that way before. He'd never known a woman who was so damn lovable—in every way. What the hell was he going to do with his life when she wasn't in it anymore?

But he couldn't think that way. Last night was the last night. It had to be. And things were going to change. He was going to be ruthless once they got back to the States. He knew he had to be.

The problem was how to go about it. He didn't seem to be very good at this stuff anymore. He should probably start giving himself little lectures, maybe on the hour, just to get ready to be tough. Maybe he could get tapes to listen to, something on stiffening his backbone. Or wiping out blocks of memory in his head. Perhaps even a prefrontal lobotomy would be called for. Yeah. That was a good idea. After all, falling in love was a form of mental illness.

Not that he was in love. No way.

But he was crazy about her. He couldn't deny that. And he was going to savor every moment of this long drive, this last long day. Because that was all he had left.

It was late evening when they crossed the border at Mexicali. They were lucky. With David's California plates, the guards didn't even ask to see ID for once, and they didn't have to bother getting Shelley a new tourist card.

It felt good to be back home, cruising California freeways again. Shelley felt excited as the La Jolla off ramps began to appear on the freeway signs.

Home. There was such comfort in the word.

A few minutes on a winding road, and there was the ocean, shimmering in the silver light of the moon.

"It's right up here to the left," she told David, sitting on the edge of her seat, anticipating the sight of her parents' house.

And there it was, looking long and low from the street. You couldn't tell from that vantage point that it went down three stories along the front of the cliff, jutting out over the waves as they hit the rocks below.

"We're here." She turned and looked at David, her eyes shining. He'd done it. Her hero.

She knew Armand was still out there somewhere, and that he still wanted to grab the kids in order to use them to extort money out of her family, but she felt safe here. Especially with David by her side. They would find a way to keep Armand at bay. She was sure of it.

Her hand curled around his. "Thank you, David. Thank you so much."

His eyes were curiously emotionless, and he didn't answer. "Let's get the kids out," he said crisply, slipping his hand out of hers and turning to open the car door.

She drew back, not sure why he was rebuffing her this way. "Sure," she said and got out as well, reaching for Jill, while David gathered Chris into his arms.

She didn't have her key to get through the security gate, so she had to ring for one of the maids. Ilsa appeared in her terry cloth robe, rubbing her eyes.

"Miss Brittman, what on earth? We weren't expecting you to come back so soon."

"Sorry I didn't call you, Ilsa. It was a sudden decision to return."

"I see." Ilsa's sharp gray eyes took in David with Chris clinging to him and she nodded. "Shall I take the children up?"

"No, you go right on back to bed, Ilsa. We'll take care of things."

"If you're sure..."

"Please. And I'm sorry I had to wake you."

"No trouble at all. We're glad to have you back, miss."

"Servants?" David noted dryly as Ilsa disappeared down a corridor.

Shelley barely gave him a glance. "Of course, servants. How could we run this huge house without them?"

"How many?"

"Three. That includes the gardener."

"Three servants to take care of the three of you?" His eyebrow rose. "Doesn't that seem a little weird to you?"

"Oh, here we go again." She led the way up the stairs to the children's rooms. "They're not here to take care of us so much as they're here to take care of the house. They have to be here even if we're not."

She opened the door to Jill's room and led her to her bed, pushing back the covers and swinging her legs under them.

In response to her last statement, David made a noise that wasn't very polite. She felt her jaw tighten. It was late. She was tired. And she was definitely losing her temper.

Whirling, she confronted him, sparks in her eyes. "What do you want me to do, throw them out on their ears? Then you could call me a cold and unfeeling exploiter of labor. At least this way they have jobs."

Turning, she started toward Chris's room.

"Ah yes, the old trickle-down theory." David came behind.

"Trickle-down jobs are better than no jobs at all."

She stopped, catching her breath. Here they were, snapping at each other. She put a hand to her forehead. "Come on, let's get Chris to bed. Then we can talk."

David looked at her, his eyes flat, like tinted glass. "I don't think we'll have any time to talk," he said evenly. "I want to get home myself."

She looked at him in surprise. She'd just assumed . . .

"You won't stay here tonight?" she asked.

"No."

"Oh." She frowned. She should have expected that, she supposed. After all, he had his life, too.

Chris was stirring in David's arms. She opened the door to his room and turned back his covers, and David laid him down, bending to kiss his forehead before he straightened again, looking down at him with a strange expression on his face.

The move surprised Shelley, but then, everything he was doing was surprising her, ever since they'd arrived in La Jolla.

He followed her out into the hallway and stopped her with a hand on her arm. "Get your locks changed, Shelley," he said calmly. "Do it first thing in the morning. Remember, Armand has your purse and everything that's in it."

She nodded, that was good advice, but there was something about the way he was giving it that she didn't like.

"And one more thing," he said, his eyes distant, like a stranger. "You need a man, Shelley. Someone to take care of you and the kids. I'd feel a lot better if you had a man around."

She reached out and put her hand softly against his chest, looking up at him. "Aren't you a man?" she said, searching his eyes.

His hand covered hers and slowly pulled it away. "I'm not the right man, Shelley, and you know it."

Her heart fell. Suddenly she realized what was going on here. Her breath caught in her throat and a sense of dread filled her body. "You're not coming back, are you?" she asked him.

He stared at her for a long moment, and then he shook his head. "No," he said coolly. "I'm not."

Tears were stinging behind her eyes, but she couldn't let him see. She forced herself to smile. "I'm sorry," she said, amazed that her voice could be so steady when her heart was breaking. "I thought we made a good team."

Before he could answer, the door to Chris's room opened and the little boy stumbled out into the hallway, blinking his sleepy eyes. "David." He put up his arms to be lifted.

David hesitated a moment, but he pulled Chris up and gave him a hug. "Good night, kid," he said gruffly. "You get back in bed, okay?"

Chris swung around and looked at his mother. "Mama? What room is David going to sleep in?"

Tears were suddenly threatening and Shelley blinked hard to hold them back. "David isn't going to have a room, Chris."

Chris shook his head, uncomprehending. "There's lots of space in my room. He could stay there." He swung back and stared into David's eyes, his own wide and innocent. "You could sleep over."

There was an odd look to David's face, and when he spoke, his voice was curiously choked. "Thanks, kid, but I've got to get back to my own place." He kicked the door open and carried Chris back to bed, tucking him in snugly and kissing him again.

Chris stared up at him. "Will you come back tomorrow?" he asked.

David hesitated, then swung away. "Maybe you ought to give old Cubby a call and have him come over real soon," he suggested to Shelley as he started across the room.

Chris's lower lip was trembling. His pudgy little fingers were clutching the covers. "I don't want Cubby," he said, his voice shaking. "David, I want you. Don't go." He sat up, the light of a new idea shining in his eyes. "Could you watch me on my bike?"

"One of these days," David said, his voice muffled.

"In the morning?"

He grimaced. "You get that head down and get some sleep, kid. We'll talk about it some other time. Okay?"

"Okay." Chris's head slipped back against the pillow. "Mama, don't let David go," he murmured sleepily. "Okay?"

David coughed. "Good night, Chris. I'm going to turn off the light."

His face had a look of desperation as he turned away from Chris's door. "I've got to get out of here," he muttered, starting to go. But Jill was standing in the doorway of her own room, and he was going to have to get past her to leave. Evidently, she had heard most of what was going on. Her face was set, showing no emotion. Shelley bit her lip. The girl was so much like her.

David looked at her, his head going back, his face hardening. He tried to walk on by, but she stepped out and stopped him.

"Do you have to go?" she asked, putting out her hand to take his. "Will you come back?"

David swallowed hard and tried to smile at her. "I'll see you again one of these days, Jill. You get back to bed."

But she wouldn't let go of his hand. "Do you think maybe you could baby-sit us again when Mama goes out?" she asked, her blue eyes luminous in the shadows. "We could come to your house." She shook her head. "We would mind you, honest. We wouldn't be bad."

David threw Shelley a trapped look and bent to kiss Jill's head. "I don't know about that, Jill. We'll see," he said huskily. "Good night, now," he muttered, pulling his hand out of hers, and then he turned, escaping down the stairs.

Shelley watched him go with a lump in her throat, but she still couldn't give vent to her emotions, not with her daughter standing so close, looking up at her.

"Come on, Jill, back to bed," she said with as much cheer as she could muster.

Jill didn't say a word. She looked into her mother's face and seemed to read exactly what was going on. Silently, she did as her mother said and slipped under the covers.

"Good night, sweetheart," Shelley said, turning off her light and closing her door.

And then she stood for a long time in the hallway, leaning against the wall, steadying herself for a future without David.

Maybe it was just as well. After all, she hardly knew the man. Falling in love so quickly had its drawbacks. But it had its advantages, too, when things didn't work out. She hadn't made any major life-style changes based on loving him. This one should be relatively easy to get over.

But as she walked slowly to her room she knew she was kidding herself. She knew she was never going to be quite the same again.

As David drove away, a dark emptiness seemed to swallow him up, and he knew why. He'd left something behind— a very important part of his spiritual anatomy.

But—no matter. The weeks ahead would be full of all sorts of activities, and he would forget about these past few days, forget about Shelley and her children. He had a business to run, a career to pursue, a life to get back into. Once he got rolling again the days would fly by. No real problem.

The trouble was, as he found out over the next week, the days didn't fly at all. They trudged, like toddlers in snowshoes. Every day seemed to last a week. Every minute he was awake, he thought about Shelley. And when he went to sleep, she was in his dreams.

His grandparents called a few days after he got back, and he apologized for having to close the café, but they would hear none of it.

"And the girl?" his grandmother asked eagerly when she took her turn on the phone. "Rosa says she's beautiful."

"What girl?" he said, trying to avoid the issue.

"The girl with the *niños*. Rosa told us all about her."

"Then you already know what she looks like."

"I just want to hear what you think she looks like."

"Okay," he said grudgingly. "She's beautiful."

"Ah, so you liked her, eh?"

"I didn't say that. I haven't seen her since I got back."

"Oh." The disappointment in his grandmother's voice was hard to take. He could have told her he'd given up his professional career to become an itinerant surfer, and she wouldn't have shown as much regret.

He changed the subject, but the sense of disappointment lingered in the air, and finally, after he hung up, he realized it was as much his own as his grandmother's.

But that was just too damn bad. He was an adult, and he would get over it. He threw himself into his work, getting to the office at dawn, staying until midnight, ignoring his friends, barking at his employees.

And then, a few days later, he saw her, purely by accident. He'd gone over to the University of California campus to participate in bidding on a landscaping project, and she was coming out of the building that he knew was named for one of her uncles. He was with two of his employees, wearing his best suit and sunglasses, and she was like a ray of sunshine surrounded by politicians and administration types. Evidently she'd just been involved in some sort of dedication ceremony. He saw her in the midst of the group coming toward him across the green, and his heart stood still.

She was so beautiful, dressed in a soft cotton suit and white gloves with her blond hair in a twist. She looked like a princess, someone royal, and that was the way the men around her were relating to her.

He stopped, watching her come closer. She looked up at the last moment and saw him.

"David," she said, reaching out. He barely touched her gloved hand, and then she was moving on, being swept along by the group she was in. She looked back. "Call me," she said, and her eyes had a look as haunted as they'd had that first night in Mexico.

But maybe that was just his imagination. Or better yet, his wishful thinking. Because that was exactly how he was feeling. Haunted. Only she couldn't see his eyes. Lucky he'd worn his sunglasses.

At any rate he called back as she was disappearing, "Sure," as though he would call. But he wouldn't. He couldn't.

And yet he did. One night, at ten o'clock, he was going nuts thinking about her, pacing the room, looking out at the traffic on the highway, drinking too much. He couldn't stop thinking about her voice, that low, silky wave of seduction that was so uniquely her own. He had to hear her voice one more time.

He dialed her number and waited for her to answer the telephone, his heart beating so hard he was sure she would hear it across the wire. She answered and he didn't say a word, finally hanging up and glaring at himself in the mirror.

"Great. Now you've sunk to terrorizing her for your own amusement."

This had to stop. He had to get out of this shell and become a real human being again. He took his friend Mitch up on an offer to double with him and his cousin from Dallas. She was a beauty—raven-haired, statuesque, funny. They went dining and dancing and he actually had a pretty good time, but when she made an obvious suggestion about coming up to her hotel room for a drink, he turned her down without a second thought. The very idea of making love to another woman didn't seem possible anymore.

Valentine's Day was coming and for the first time in his life, he was paying attention to it. How could he help it? Everywhere he looked someone was trumpeting the coming holiday. Funny—in years past, he'd never thought twice about Valentine's Day. He'd always considered it sort of a made-up holiday, something the card companies had invented to sell cards. But this year was different. He found himself buying things—a huge box of chocolates shaped in a heart, a stuffed cat with a big satin heart attached to its neck that he knew Jill would love, and a red fire engine for Chris. Then a stuffed bunny, and a cute little turtle with ears that wiggled. And cards—big, lacy cards with hearts and arrows and mushy sentiments that made him cringe.

Why was he buying these things? It was a compulsion. He couldn't stop himself. Soon he had stacks of cards and candy and stuffed animals at his condominium. Any more of this and he was going to have to rent another room for storage of all this junk.

What was he going to do with it? His trash can was going to look pretty silly on the fifteenth of February.

He wanted to be himself again, to go back to what he'd been like before he'd ever met Shelley, but it didn't seem to be possible. At first he thought time would do the trick. But time wasn't working. Nothing was.

Even his secretary was beginning to notice that he'd changed. "I've just about had it with you," she told him one afternoon.

He looked up from his desk with a frown. "What do you mean?"

"You're so tense." She shook her auburn curls and looked him over. "You know what you need?"

He threw down his pen and leaned back in his chair. "I hate to ask, but I know you'll tell me anyway."

"You need to find a woman and settle down."

"What?" He felt as though she'd jolted him with an electric shock. How could she say such a thing? They'd known each other for years. She knew how he felt about these things. "Try again, Doris. No cigar on this one."

"No, I mean it." She perched on the corner of his desk and looked at him pityingly. "You need someone to take care of you, David. I can read the signs."

"I can get a housekeeper for that."

"That's not the kind of care I'm talking about." She squinted at him. "Besides, that's not all you need. You need someone to take care of, too. It works both ways, David. Trust me. Gregg and I've been married for fifteen years. I know."

She got up and left his office and didn't mention it again, but her advice stuck with him, anyway. He kept remembering that almost the last thing he'd said to Shelley was, "You need a man to take care of you." Only he'd opted out of being that man.

He'd been driving past her house. He had to do it. He had to make sure she was okay, though what he was going to learn from the street he wasn't sure. He saw the kids once, Jill, with her journal under her arm, disappearing into the house and Chris running in behind her, yelling, "Don't step on my..."

He didn't know what Jill wasn't supposed to step on, but the sight and sound of them brought memories back in a wave, and his eyes were stinging as he drove on.

And then it was Valentine's Day. It had become a sort of milestone in his mind. He kept thinking that if he could just get through Valentine's Day, he would be over the hump. Things could start getting back to normal.

But just because it was Valentine's Day he had to drive by her house one last time. It was early in the morning when he got into his car and started toward La Jolla. He wanted to catch Shelley coming out with the kids. Just one long look. That was all he wanted.

He drove by slowly, glancing to the right, but there wasn't a sign of life at the house. No one was in sight.

A tiger-striped cat ran out suddenly from behind a parked car and he stepped on the brakes to avoid it. At the same time his gaze strayed to the left side of the road. What he saw chilled him to the bone. A small black van was parked there. Two men were sitting in the front seats. Though he only got a glimpse, he was sure one of those men was Armand.

Armand. Someone must have smuggled him across the border. Obviously he was getting desperate enough about getting hold of those kids to risk being arrested.

Hoping against hope that they hadn't recognized him, he raced his car down the street and around the corner of the next block to a convenience store, skidding to a stop at the telephone booth. Vaulting out of his car, he plunked a quarter in the slot and called 911.

"This is David Coronado." He gave them his address. "I want to report a kidnapping attempt being made." He related the pertinent information as quickly as he could, his heart thumping. "I've got to get back and see what's going on," he said at last, impatient with their questions. "Get here as fast as you can!"

He drove back one block and parked, getting out to walk the rest of the way. Just as he came into view, he saw the front door of the house open. Chris bounced out, followed by Jill at a more stately pace, and then Shelley. At the same time he could see the doors of the black van beginning to open.

He started to run. He couldn't tackle both men at once, but he could put a crimp in their style.

"Shelley," he yelled as he ran. "Get the kids back in the house. Now!"

But it took her a few seconds to understand what was going on, and in those few seconds, Chris and Jill saw him.

"David!" Chris yelled, and began to run toward him as fast as his little legs would take him.

Jill was almost as quick as Shelley to realize the situation. "No, Chris!" she called, running out to catch him.

He was too fast for her. "David, David!" he called, still coming, still running right into danger.

They were all coming out into the street, all doing exactly what they shouldn't be doing, all putting themselves in harm's way. It was too late to stop them now. He had to stop Armand.

Both men were out of the van; both running toward the children. Armand was closest, and David hurled himself at the man. It felt as though he was flying. Just before he hit, he caught sight of a flash of metal, and he knew Armand was armed. And then he had Armand by the legs, toppling him to the ground, and they both fell with a bone-crunching thud to the pavement where he struck his cheek.

Wrestling had never been his strong suit, but the will to win was strong enough to make up for that. Armand was grunting, trying to turn him, but he held the man and he heard the gun clatter away onto the street. Dimly, out of the corner of his eye, he could see that the accomplice had turned back to help Armand.

"Run, Shelley. Grab the kids and run," he managed to yell out just before the man's foot hit his head and everything went black.

But only for a moment. He shook his head and his eyes cleared enough to see that Shelley did have the kids and she was hauling them back into the house. Relief swept through him, relief that grew as he detected the sound of sirens coming their way. It was okay. Now all he had to do was hold on and make sure these two bastards didn't get away before the cops got here. It was going to be okay.

"Hold still." Shelley dabbed David's face with antiseptic.

"Ouch!" He pulled away. "Hey, that stings."

"Oooh, big brave man," she teased, her eyes full of emotion despite her light tone. "You can tackle two bad guys with a single blow, but when it comes to a little topical pain..."

"*Little* is a relative term," he grumbled, frowning. "When you have a sadistic nurse probing your wounds to find out what hurts..."

"Watch out or I'll give you a sponge bath," she said crisply, dabbing again. "Nurse is in charge, you know."

He couldn't help but grin. "Is that a threat or a promise?"

Their eyes met and the grin faded, and Shelley turned away, packing up her implements of torture. "The kids think you're a hero," she said softly. "Jill is upgrading you in her journal."

As if on cue the children came charging into the room. Chris launched himself into David's lap and Jill hung back, a little more shyly, but touching his sleeve.

"Thank you for saving us, David," she said quietly.

Reaching out, he pulled her into his lap, as well, ignoring the pain. Looking down into the girl's blue eyes, he remembered her question to him that first day in Mexico, when she'd told him she didn't really like her father. "Is that bad?" she'd asked him. And now she'd seen her father dragged away by the police in the midst of attempting to kidnap her.

His heart went out to Jill. He'd thought he had problems with his parents' separation. The magnitude of Jill's eclipsed his. But he had been in some of the places she was going. Whatever else happened in his life, he suddenly made a silent vow to keep in touch with Jill. She was going to need someone to talk to, someone who could help put these things into perspective for her. He wouldn't trust that job to anyone else. Somehow he knew it had to be his.

"Can you watch me ride my tricycle now?" Chris asked, bouncing in his lap.

David grinned. Chris wasn't going to need as much help as Jill. But he wanted to be there for the boy, too. If he needed a man to watch him as he achieved the turning points in his life, why couldn't it be him?

"I'll watch you, Chris. I've been looking forward to it."

Shelley hid her smile and patted her son on the head.

"Okay, you two, go down to the playroom. We'll be down in a few minutes." She turned anxiously as the children be-

gan to leave the room. "But don't open the sl
patio until we get there, Chris. Stay inside. Okay?

David looked at her and shook his head. "Don   ,,
Shelley. Armand's been arrested. And from what the detective said, they should have enough on him to lock him away for a while, and probably get him deported. I don't think you'll have to worry about that jerk again for a long time."

She folded her arms and shivered slightly, her eyes dark with remembered pain. Rising again, she stood over where he was sitting, looking restless. "That was so close, David. I don't ever want to feel so frightened again."

That brought up subjects he didn't feel prepared to deal with. He wanted to take her in his arms, hold her close, never let her go. But he didn't have a right to. "I'm just glad I was here at the right time," he murmured, looking away.

She turned back and stared down at him. "That brings up an interesting question. Just exactly what were you doing here?" she asked, her eyes sparkling.

He glanced up and tried to look innocent. "Who, me?"

Her smile was beginning to show. "Yes, you."

He shrugged, eyes wide. "Driving by."

"I see. Is this on your route to work?"

He grimaced and tried not to smile. "Sometimes."

She gave a short laugh. "How can it be, David? It's got to be miles out of your way." She poked him with her foot. "Come on. Fess up now. What were you doing?" There was hope in her face.

His gaze tangled with hers and held. "Checking on you," he admitted at last.

She was melting inside. "Why?" she asked softly, holding his gaze.

He couldn't tell her. If he told her, he was doomed. Staggering a little, he stood up and turned to get out of there as quickly as he could. But she wasn't going to let him go so easily. Standing in his way, she looked up into his eyes.

"David," she said, her voice shaking ever so slightly. "I have to tell you something. I can't let you just walk out of our lives again without saying it."

He shook his head, wanting to back away, but she had him cornered.

"Don't look at me that way," she said, biting her lip. "This isn't easy. But I have to do it."

She swallowed hard, looking down as though gathering strength and then raising her eyes again, brave, but scared.

"David, when I first met you, I thought you were awfully attractive, but sort of messed up. You seemed to have a grudge against me or something. I couldn't figure it out. But the more you seemed to shy away, the more I wanted to get to know you."

She turned away and walked toward the window, her arms folded, her shoulders tense. He knew he should take this opportunity to escape, but he couldn't move, except to follow her. He stood behind her, and they both looked out on the waves in the blue gray ocean.

"You kissed me and it opened up a whole new aspect to our relationship. I...I had a very severe crush on you." She glanced back at him, stifling a smile, a little embarrassed. "And when we made love, it only got worse."

He took her shoulders in his hands, leaning in to breathe the scent of her hair, and she leaned back against him, sighing with the feel of his body against hers, relaxing at last. But she still avoided his eyes, staring out at the sea.

"David, I knew I liked you a lot, more than any man, ever. But I didn't realize I was...in love with you until that night at the motel in Mexico."

He started to say something, but she turned, putting a finger to his lips.

"I know you don't want to marry me," she said with tears trembling in her eyes. "You don't have to explain all of that again. But I think you like me. Don't you? So why can't we be together for a while?"

He couldn't speak, but his arms came around her, even as he was shaking his head, trying to deny what he knew had to happen.

"I love you, David," she whispered, searching his eyes for an answering emotion. Her hand grazed his cheek. "I love you."

His lips touched hers hungrily, and his body betrayed his good intentions. She arched up into his embrace, and he pulled her close, loving the way she clung to him, needing to feel her touch as he needed life.

And at the same time, he was in agony. Here he was so afraid of being hurt, and yet he'd never been in as much pain as he'd suffered through these past few days without her. It was too late to save himself. He was in love with her. And there was nothing he could do about it.

But that wasn't true. There was something he could do about it.

Drawing back, he looked into her eyes. "I love you, too, Shelley," he murmured as though it were the confession of a crime. "You must know that."

She smiled through her tears, and he kissed her again, groaning. "But love isn't the issue, Shelley. Love isn't the end of the story."

"It is for me," she said simply, her hand cradling his cheek, love shining in her eyes. "I've loved you forever, I think."

He smiled down at her. How could he resist? "I've been in love with you from the moment I first heard your voice."

She laughed, blinking away the dampness. "Oh, I see. Isn't that something new? Love at first sound."

He laughed, then sobered again, the frown coming back with his doubts. "My parents loved each other, too. And look what happened to them."

She wouldn't retreat. "We're not your parents." She sighed. "Oh, David, don't you see? You owe it to us to see what we could do together." She stood on tiptoe and kissed his mouth. "I think you're going to be surprised," she said softly.

She was so beautiful, so adorable. What was he torturing himself for? This was what he wanted. This was more than he deserved, more than he'd ever dreamed he could have. Why not reach for it now?

A sense of wonder surged inside him, flooding every nerve, every pore. It was all right to love Shelley. There was nothing wrong with it. He wanted her so badly he could taste it in his choked throat. And yet he still couldn't get rid of his misgivings. "Shelley, your entire life-style is so different from mine."

"My life-style is changing, David. Don't you understand that?" She touched his cheek again, her eyes yearning into his. "Don't you see that I'm not happy with the life-style I've lived all these years? I've spent most of my life searching for something else. I've already made arrangements to go into business with my friend. And I'm looking at houses to move my kids into. I don't want this one anymore. I'm ready to move on."

More ready than he was, it seemed. More brave. More wonderful. Suddenly he had to laugh at himself.

"What a wimp," he muttered, shaking his head.

"Are you going to start calling me names now?" she asked.

"I'm not talking about you. I'm talking about me." He laughed shortly. "I've been petrified by fear ever since I met you."

"Fear of what?"

"Fear of falling in love with you." He grinned, saying it again. "What a wimp. I didn't even know that what I was resisting was the best thing that could ever happen to me."

She kissed him again. "And you're not going to resist any longer—are you?"

No. He really wasn't. He held her close and breathed in her scent. He was finally going to allow himself to be happy. It was the best feeling he'd ever had.

"It's funny," she said softly, her head to his chest, feeling contentment for the first time in many days. "I'll bet you don't even know what day today is."

He knew what she was driving at, and he grinned. "The fourteenth of February. Why?"

She laughed. "Oh, never mind, David. It doesn't matter. It's only that it's Valentine's Day."

"Ah, yes."

She shook her head, looking at him with love. "You're just not very romantic, are you?"

"I guess not." He sighed. "Things like Valentine's Day are way over my head."

"Beast," she muttered.

He suppressed a grin, thinking about the stacks of cards and presents he had stashed away at home. "Listen, right after we watch Chris on his tricycle, pack up the kids. Let's go over to my place. I have something I want to show you." He could hardly wait to see her face when she saw how wrong she was. *Beast,* indeed.

She looked up at him, not letting go, but not sure if she could trust this yet. "So you're willing to give us a try?"

"No." He stared down at her, then curled her more tightly into his arms. "Not just a try, Shelley. We're going to make it together, you and me."

"And the kids," she added, her eyes shining.

"And the kids," he vowed from his heart, and he sealed it with a kiss.

The valentines would just have to come later.

* * * * *

SILHOUETTE® *Desire®*

MYSTERY MATES!

Six sexy Bachelors explosively pair with six sultry Bachelorettes to find the Valentine's surprise of a lifetime.

Get to know the mysterious men who breeze into the lives of these unsuspecting women. Slowly uncover—as the heroines themselves must do—the missing pieces of the puzzle that add up to hot, *hot* heroes! You begin by knowing nothing about these enigmatic men, but soon you'll know *everything....*

Heat up your winter with:

#763   THE COWBOY by Cait London

#764   THE STRANGER by Ryanne Corey

#765   THE RESCUER by Peggy Moreland

#766   THE WANDERER by Beverly Barton

#767   THE COP by Karen Leabo

#768   THE BACHELOR by Raye Morgan

Mystery Mates—coming in February from Silhouette Desire. Because you never know who you'll meet....

Take 4 bestselling love stories FREE

Plus get a FREE surprise gift!

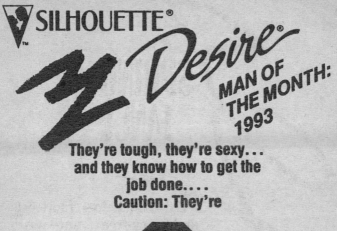